LOVE DEVIOUS

MOHSEN HEDAYATI

Order this book online at www.trafford.com
or email orders@trafford.com

Most Trafford titles are also available at major online book retailers.

Hasan Tarkhani (painter of cover)l

Printed in Victoria, BC, Canada.

ISBN: 978-1-4269-1740-0 (Soft)
ISBN: 978-1-4269-1741-7 (Hard)

Library of Congress Control Number: 2009940290

Our mission is to efficiently provide the world's finest, most comprehensive book publishing service, enabling every author to experience success. To find out how to publish your book, your way, and have it available worldwide, visit us online at www.trafford.com

Trafford rev. 11/25/2009

www.trafford.com

North America & international
toll-free: 1 888 232 4444 (USA & Canada)
phone: 250 383 6864 ♦ fax: 812 355 4082

To My
Parents
Whom I adore.

Contents

Chapter 1

The people of the village were in their usual, calm, and night sleep, and the bright moon had made a beautiful scene in the small village. Stars were awake all night. Everything was in utter silence, but it didn't abide until morning and everything changed in two shakes.

The sky of the village was getting darker and the moon was disappearing behind dark clouds. Some tremulous sounds were being heard and they were increasing momentarily, but still all people were asleep deeply. The farmer was dreaming about his farm and animals.

There was a high mountain in the northern part of the village and it was covered by dim clouds. There was huge mist above the summit of the mountain. There were strange sounds around the village. It wasn't clear what was about to happen. By higher rise of the terrible sounds, people got up while taken aback and they came out of their houses to find out what was happening around them. They were all panicked.

After a while, the earth started to tremble very slowly. It made people more and more frightened, and now, women and children were awake, too. Some people thought about an earthquake, others about a flood and the others about any horrible events that could be imagined.

Passing time, sounds were getting more dreadful. All tiny kids, girls, and women were screaming. Men and especially the elderly were doing their best to make others calm and give peace to village, but they were, too, threatened. It was believed that the elderly knew some about this terrible event.

Everything was exactly like fifty years ago. When these old men were young, a volcano erupted on the north of the village and made an earthly hell through beautiful tall trees and colorful flowers. This demonic event did not show mercy toward children, women, nor men. It just swallowed what-whosever resisting against it with an insatiate hunger.

An event that ignited all hearts; all those burnt in magma and even those burnt owing to losing their relatives, and unfortunately maybe their loves; lovers that could love their beloved some more hours ….

And tonight, history felt like renewing after fifty years of flourishing. The peak of the mountain was getting red and yellow releasing magma. A paroxysm of igneous melted materials was sloping down to earth, but shrieks of people were ascending upper and upper to the heaven.

All people were calling God from the depth of their hearts; each in their own words to save them from this calamity; as people mostly remember God in the calamities. They were all running to the south. There was a long wide river along the village which divided it into two northern and southern parts. If they could pass the river, they could save themselves. What a beautiful river it was! It was the border of life and death. There were just meters and seconds between life and death.

It was a shiny red night and there wasn't any sign of darkness anymore. This time, being light was worse than being dark. Red, orange, and yellow had made the box of colored pencils that night. No other sounds were heard but loud screams. Who knew where the night swallows were that night; birds which sang all night long before.

People in the southern part were safe because melted materials couldn't cross the river, and they were helping other people on the other side, but the northern part was nearly covered with igneous magma. Boats were taking people to the other side of the river as fast as they could. Priority was with children and women. They were the first to cross the river. Boats were few and small and they couldn't transport many people in each crossing.

Mr. Oliver took his two children, ran toward the boat rapidly, and left them inside it. Edgar closed his sister's eyes firmly with his hands.

Mr. Oliver surged back to save his wife; his love, his Venus who awaited him, but it was too late. He faced an unbelievable scene in front of his eyes. Venus's feet had drawn in magma and she was screaming loudly.

Mr. Oliver couldn't halt himself and ran to Venus with no doubt because the warmth of his love to Venus was million times more than the heat of that magma. He ran toward his love and took her hand and tried to get her, but they got besieged by magma and cried together loudly. The word of love could be easily heard from their shout.

Poor Edgar and Lisa heard their parents' love word from beyond the river.

Poor children now just could see fire and ashes, fog and mist, red and yellow. They could see everything except their parents, their house, and their small garden. There was nothing except nothing. Lisa was too child to discern anything, but Edgar was completely shocked and didn't know what to do. He couldn't believe anything yet. Some shiny small tears were rolling down from the lake of his eyes. He wished he could cry as much as he could extinguish the whole fire and save everybody especially his mom and dad.

One cart carried children to the next village to keep them far away from that hell. Edgar and his sister were in that cart. The cart driver, who was an old man, drove as fast as he could, to keep children aloof from there because he didn't want to let them see that horrible environment anymore. The cart was full of small children who were crying. They all were thinking of their parents and families. Their tiny eyes were all wet. In the path, after about one mile, one of the boys jumped out of the cart and ran toward the village. The cart driver stopped to catch him, but the boy ran as fast as he could and disappeared in the darkness of night into woods. The carter came back to the cart and went on driving to the next village.

Lisa was asleep in her brother's bosom. She didn't know what had happened and what was going on around her. She couldn't understand the situation. She was sleeping deeply in utter innocence. But instead, her brother's eyes were open even with no wink and there was a big mask of silence on his mien. It was clear he was fully shocked and astonished. He didn't want to believe what had happened to him and his little sister. He couldn't believe being apart from his parents who always were beside him and Lisa. He looked strangely at the children in the cart; they all shared the same destiny. He was just ten years old and now he had to take care of his 4-year-old sister.

Heavy dark clouds started to rain smoothly. Maybe they cried for this harrowing event and thunders' roar held a sense of anger. The cart didn't have any roof and poor children got wet. Edgar took out his coat and dragged it on Lisa pressing her hands firmly to keep her warm. She was still asleep and her beautiful round eyes were off. She had a very strange smile on her lips. Maybe she thought she was sleeping in her mother's kind, warm bosom.

The shiny sun was emerging little by little from behind the mountains. It was very shiny and happy as usual. It made a light curtain behind children's eyelid.

They had just arrived at their destination. It was a very big village which was completely different from that of their own. Edgar hadn't been there before and it was strange for him. But he had heard about it from his father.

The cart stopped in front of the office of the sheriff. The old cart driver went inside and left the children outside. Children were to be kept there for as long as their own village got restored again.

Edgar woke up Lisa by a kiss on her pale cheek. She woke up and sat quietly for a moment looking at Edgar and other children. Everything was unknown for her. It seemed that she was a bit frightened. She went to Edgar's bosom and hugged him firmly. Edgar took him and they got off from the cart.

"Where is Mom?" asked Lisa curiously.

Edgar was silent and he didn't know what to say. He looked at her and then thought again.

But Lisa didn't keep silent and asked again, "Where is Dad?"

Edgar took her hands and they walked near to a narrow stream and sat beside it on the grass. Limpid water passed the narrow stream. He made a smile and looked kindly at her sister.

"They are ..." Edgar muttered, "they're in heaven, Lisa. They will live there, after this." answered Edgar with a drop of tear rolling down from his eyes.

"But, you are crying!" said Lisa sorrowfully.

"No... no, I'm not crying" replied Edgar and made a fake smile on his lips.

Lisa didn't perceive what Edgar spoke about. She started playing with water since she liked it very much. She followed the stream and went down along the water.

There were a lot of bushes of raspberry around them. Edgar picked some raspberries from the bush beside them and gave all to Lisa. She loved raspberries a lot and got busy eating them. Edgar was happy seeing his sister glad. After eating raspberries, she stood up and ran on the grass. Edgar followed her, and so, they played. They ran into the beautiful jungle around them and followed each other through the woods.

All of a sudden, Edgar remembered that they had left the cart for quite a while. He looked around him, but he couldn't find the path they took. He got very disturbed whereas his tiny sister laughed and played in the woods. He looked again around him more carefully. They had lost the stream, and going further in, they entered another side of the village. All around them were houses and cottages and they were inside the crowd of people. All people looked strangely at Edgar and a little girl beside him. They walked through the alleys for a while but couldn't find the cart. Edgar was again silent. He didn't know anybody in that big village. They were lost.

He thought and thought, but didn't find any place to go. They didn't have any relatives in their own village or in their neighboring village. In the midst of thinking, Edgar suddenly found that his father had a very good and close friend, called Mr. Jackson, in that village. His father always told them about Mr. Jackson and he always said that he lived in the next village which is very big. So, Edgar thought that Mr. Jackson would be in that village.

Mr. Jackson was a successful businessman in his region and he was famous for his beneficent manner toward poor people. He loved Edgar and Lisa so much that he always gave a lot of gifts to them when he went to visit them. When Edgar was about 7 years old, Mr. Jackson had given him a beautiful and precious necklace with a silver round plaque and another one to his sister. Both necklaces were the same, even their round plaques. On their plaques had drawn a picture of rose flower. At that time, Lisa was only one year old.

Edgar took out his necklace and stared at it for a while and sighed. He hoped to find Mr. Jackson and count on him. He took Lisa's hand and started looking for Mr. Jackson's address. They asked people about his address. His guess was true. His father's friend lived there and, since he was famous, everybody knew him. So, they could soon find his house asking people. Now, there was a sweet smile on Edgar's lips and a sign of hope in his shiny eyes.

Finally, they found Mr. Jackson's house. His house was far away from the center of the village near woods. It was a beautiful and big house surrounded by old trees all around it. In the yard, there were different kinds of plants and colorful flowers, but they were not fresh and lush as if no one had watered them a long time.

Edgar knocked at the door and waited behind it hopefully. He looked at Lisa and cracked a smile. After a while, someone unlocked the door. A young boy with disheveled, blond hair and slack body came out, as if he felt no pain. He had rude eyes and a big nose. He stood up in front of the children scratching his untidy hair. Edgar got shocked and Lisa hid behind him because she was afraid of that coarse and ugly boy.

"Yes? What do you two want?" shouted the boy violently.

"Sorry, I am looking for Mr. Jackson, am I right?" answered Edgar in a small voice.

The boy could hardly hear them. He scrutinized them and stared at Edgar. Then, he answered in a very rough voice, "There is no Mr. Jackson any longer; he died four months ago, and you poor people can go and find another Mr. Jackson for yourself to give you food and clothes. We don't have any beneficent person in this house anymore. Now get you gone and never disturb me again."

Edgar got very sad and nervous; he wanted to say that they were not beggars, but the cruel boy banged the door. Lisa was still behind her brother, her legs wobbly from panic. It seemed that there was no trace of kind Mr. Jackson. There was just one cruel and impolite boy; a memento from him. Who could believe a gentleman like Mr. Jackson could have such a stupid son? But sometimes, children are not the followers of their parents. If all children followed their parents' manner, nothing would have changed in this world.

Edgar again got very sad and hopeless facing that despairing event. They walked through allies not knowing where they were going.

After minutes, Lisa became hungry. She hadn't eaten any breakfast and had walked a too long distance. She jumped in front of Edgar and asked him for something to eat. They stopped in front of a bakery and Edgar looked all his pockets for money. He could just find fifty cents in his pockets. He could afford one small chocolate cake. He was hungry too, but he knew that Lisa always is more important, so he bought a chocolate cake and gave all to Lisa. They sat on a bench beside large area of trees. Lisa ate her chocolate cake fast. Edgar was too tired and also hungry, but he was happy that his sister was eating. After a short while he closed his eyes little by little under the pressure of tiredness and hunger. He was as tired as he could sleep for long hours.

Lisa was still eating her chocolate cake veraciously. She suddenly saw a white rabbit with brown spots behind his neck drinking water in a small puddle. It was so beautiful that every child would love to hug it. So, she was tempted to go beside the rabbit and fondle it. Then she left her brother and went near the puddle. She tried to catch rabbit, but it ran away. She tried again and again, but each time she went closer to the rabbit, it escaped. She followed it wherever it ran. She fell down several times, but she was determined to catch it.

It was about noon. A mild wind was blowing in the area. It took scent of flowers to Edgar's nose and awakened him. It resembled kisses that his mother bestowed every morning to wake him up. He took a deep breath stretching his body. Then he looked around him for Lisa, but he found that she was not there. He stood up and looked all around, but he couldn't see her.

"Where can she be?" He asked himself stressfully.

He got disturbed and anxious. He looked everywhere for Lisa, but his try ended nowhere. He got more and more anxious. After that horrible event, he had no one except Lisa in the whole world. He asked every one, but no one had seen her. He was too tired and hungry and he couldn't walk anymore. His lips grew like a desert and Lisa's absence was like a burning sun that made him weaker, but he was determined to find his sister. He walked through the allies and he fell down several times, but he stood up again with the power of love. Whenever he imagined Lisa alone crying somewhere, his effort increased to find her soon. He walked not knowing where he was going. He again asked many people about Lisa, but all of them responded him by shaking their head.

He walked for hours nonstop even a moment. Hours passed and it got dark and everybody had gone to their homes and all allies and streets were silent. His feet became shorter and shorter. He could breathe hard. His lips had been shrunk. There was no strength to go on and he couldn't continue walking anymore. His eyes were getting darker. Finally his eyes had been closed and he swooned in front of a supermarket.

Next morning, when Mr. White came to open his supermarket, he found a young boy lying there.

He thought Edgar is one of the vagrants or beggars that always sleep under the balcony of the shops to be safe from rain. He tipped Edgar slowly, but the poor boy didn't move. He tried twice more, but Edgar didn't wake up and he was still unconscious. He was lay down like a corpse. Mr. White felt sorry for the poor boy, so he opened the supermarket and took him in. Then he poured some cold water on his face, but it didn't work out.

He immediately called Doctor Paul. Till doctor's arrival, Mr. White again poured some water on Edgar's face, but he didn't wake up. After about a quarter, Doctor Paul appeared and opened his bag to start his job.

"Who is he, Mr. White?" asked Doctor curiously.

"I don't know! When I came here, I found him in front of my shop, but something inside told me that he is not a beggar or even a vagrant.

I could trace some sort of innocence on his mien. Then, I respecting my intuition, took him inside and called you immediately." replied Mr. White.

"Any way, poor boy is in a very bad condition, but he is still alive. His body is very cold. You should keep him warm." said Doctor and then he did everything necessary.

"I injected some ampoules into him. Keep him warm and let him rest some hours, then he will regain his consciousness slowly. And then give these pills to him each four hours. In case of any problem, call me soon …" said Doctor Paul and gave some drugs to Mr. White and left there.

After some hours, Edgar opened his eyes while murmuring, "Lis, Lis, Lisa …"

Mr. White made his ear close to Edgar's mouth, but he didn't understand what he said. He sat beside Edgar and gave him one pill with a glass of cold water then some fruits and chocolates to make him lustier. When he got better, Mr. White started asking him some questions. While thinking about Lisa, Edgar explained everything to Mr. White from that horrible event up to Lisa's disappearance. He was speaking hard. Once he tried to stand up, but he couldn't.

"What are you doing? Just lay down" said Mr. White.

"No, I can't … I have to go and find my sister. How can I sleep here while Lisa is wandering lonely? She is only 4. She needs me." replied Edgar.

"No! You cannot even move. You are not in good condition. Doctor said you have to rest. Now lay down and sleep." said Mr. White in reply emphatically.

Edgar didn't listen to Mr. White and tried to get up, but he was disabled to move. He coughed and then felt sleepy. Mr. White was a serious man, but very kind and well-tempered. He felt pity for the poor boy and also his tiny sister, so he decided to do something for them. He thought for a while, and suddenly, came up with an idea. He found that he could keep Edgar in the shop until he could find his sister. It was a good opportunity for him, too, because he was alone in the shop and didn't have any shop-boy. When Edgar got up again and was better, Mr. White told him his suggestion and he accepted it gladly.

Since then, Edgar worked for Mr. White in his supermarket as a shop-boy. When people came shopping, he carried their goods and merchandises to their homes, and when he was in the shop, he decorated the goods and made the shop clean. He worked there every day until about four o'clock in the afternoon. Finishing his job, he went out to find his sister, Lisa. It turned a routine for days. He looked for Lisa until midnights. He asked for her everywhere, but no one knew anything. He never got disappointed and did her best to find Lisa with all his might. He wasn't pleased with the way matters were shaping, but he had to get along. He just knew that he had to find Lisa at any price as soon as possible.

Mr. White was very satisfied with Edgar and also all costumers loved him a lot as their own child. Everyone found him as a polite and active boy, but all of them could see and feel a deep sadness on his face and always they gave some money to him as a gift when he finished his work. He was really polite and silent and nothing could make him angry. His coevals played outside, but he had to work. He had to work because he had no other choices. When some silly boys saw him carrying people's goods, they mocked him and made fun of him so rudely. But Edgar didn't pay any attention to them, kept silent and did his job.

One week passed and there was no sign of Lisa. Only God knew where she was. Passing time, Edgar missed his tiny sister more and more. He dreamed Lisa all nights, but when he got up in the morning, he would drench in sadness. He looked for her everywhere possible in the village.

Edgar sat on a stone in front of the supermarket under the shadow of the balcony. He played with a small piece of wood drawing shapes on the ground. Right then, an old woman came to the shop. She was about sixty or more, but she looked very kind and well-dressed. When she entered, Mr. White greeted her in a loud voice. It was clear that he knew her very well.

"Hellooooooo, Good morning dear Mrs. Bell." said Mr. White loudly and stood up behind the cash box.

"Hi, Mr. White. It seems that you are in high spirits today. What has happened to you?" smiled Mrs. Bell.

"Yes! You are right. You know, I am getting older and weaker day by day and I couldn't control here lonely. But after a long time, I have found a very active and polite shop-boy that helps me a lot. I trust him completely. He is exactly the one I desired. He helps me very much and I do less since he has came." remarked Mr. White.

"Good. This is my shopping list; would you please collect these for me?" said Mrs. Bell and gave a piece of paper to Mr. White.

"Of course yes! Just wait a moment." answered Mr. White gently and took the list.

While he was gathering her shopping list, Mrs. Bell saw some bear-shaped chocolates and ordered Mr. White to give some to her.

"But chocolate isn't good for you dear madam. These are for kids, they love such shapes." smiled Mr. White.

"I know! But I want these cute chocolates for someone else." replied Mrs. Bell.

As Mrs. Bell lived alone, it was strange for Mr. White whom she wanted those chocolates for. Anyway, he collected everything that she needed, put them in her basket and called Edgar to carry the goods to her home. Edgar came in immediately and took the basket. It was a bit heavy for Edgar to pick up. Mrs. Bell looked at him strangely as if she knew him from somewhere before.

Anyhow, Edgar took all things and followed Mrs. Bell toward her house. It was a bit far from the supermarket. They were walking and speaking together through allies. Mrs. Bell was a kind woman and she enjoyed speaking to the young boy. She loved Edgar a lot and when they reached home she asked him to come in and take a rest. But he didn't accept. He wanted to go back to shop very soon to keep Mr. White satisfied and pleased.

When he put down the goods and wanted to go back, Mrs. Bell took three dollars out of her pocket and gave to Edgar in tip. Edgar got very happy by getting 3 dollars, because others always gave him cents. No one had given him such a big tip before.

"Thank you, madam. I hope I can requite your kindness a day." said Edgar and took the money in his fist firmly and then he ran as fast as he could toward supermarket.

On the way, he saw some boys around a corner speaking loudly. One of them in the middle was speaking loudly and others were listening to him. He was speaking about a shiny stone.

Edgar got closer and saw that one of them had found a beautiful shiny stone and he wanted to sell it to his friend. But none of his friends paid attention to his worthless stone and they mocked him rudely.

"Who would pay for that worthless stone?" said one of them and laughed loudly.

"I wouldn't pay for that worthless stone even one cent." said the other.

"If I had money I would buy something to eat." said the third.

Edgar opened his fist slowly and looked at the money that Mrs. Bell had given him. He thought that he could buy this beautiful shiny stone and give it to Lisa as a present when he found her. She would be really happy because of having this present. So, he went inside them and stood in front of the heavy boy.

"Look! Who is here? The poor shop-boy." said one of the boys and took a rude look at Edgar.

"You must be in the shop and carry people's things. What are you doing here?" said the other and they all laughed loudly at him.

Edgar got very sad at silly boys. First he changed his mind to buy the stone, because he knew that they would laugh at him. But then he remembered Lisa and it made him strong enough to dare to offer his demand.

"I buy your stone." said Edgar to the boy.

"You don't have any money. How would you buy this?" answered the heavy boy rudely.

"I do…" answered Edgar firmly.

"Oh! How much would you pay for this? My stone is very precious." answered the boy in a silly voice.

Edgar looked at his fist again and said "I… I'll pay you three dollars for that."

Everyone got surprised. They kept silent for a while. The heavy boy didn't believe himself and said "three dollars? That's okay, but I won't pay back your money if you ask latter."

Edgar agreed and the boy gave that stone to him quickly and he left there soon. When he left there, all the boys started to speak about him.

"How can a shop-boy pay three dollars for a worthless stone?" remarked one of them surprisingly.

"I am sure he is a stealer. He steals Mr. White's cash box." said a second jealously.

"I found that worthless stone from the river when I was going to fishing in Black Lake yesterday. Sun had shined on it and its sparkles drew my attention. A snake was snuck around it. No one would buy that worthless stone from me except that stupid boy!" said the owner of the stone in a very ridiculing way.

"Easy come easy go, buddy. He had stolen the money easily, so, he wasted it easily, too." said one of the boys.

"He was really simple-minded. If I were in his shoes, I would never pay three dollars for that worthless stone. I would buy some chocolates to put in my stomach, instead." said another boy laughing loudly.

All of them said something about Edgar and all together laughed at him loudly.

Edgar went back to the supermarket with a beautiful and shiny stone in his fist and he didn't show that to Mr. White because he didn't want to show it to anyone. He just wanted to give that to Lisa as a birthday present. Because it was the first of June and after five days, it would be Lisa's birthday. So, Edgar's struggle increased to find his little sister and be beside her on her birthday. He really couldn't bear her absence and he didn't like to think about possibility of any danger to her.

"Where can she be? Is she in danger now? No! Where has she been so far? Why nobody saw her anywhere?" thought Edgar.

All these were questions storming miserably in his mind. But he couldn't find any answers. Asking these questions from himself, he dreamed of about Lisa's birthday; the day of happiness.

That day was unforgettable for him. At that time he was about six years old and he was the only child of Mr. Oliver's family. His parents loved him very much, but those days, they waited a new coming baby. They all were happy for the arrival of a beautiful angel to their warm family.

Mr. Oliver had decorated the entire house with fresh and colorful roses. It was about eight o'clock in the afternoon. The sun was giving her place to moon and they were greeting with each other like every night and morning. A mild wind was blowing outside. The color of sunset had made the garden dark orange. Everything was prepared the birth of a little angel.

In last moments, his mother was suffered being in the sweetest stomachaches she had had ever in her life, because it was for her tiny Lisa. They had named the baby before her birth. She eagerly waited for Lisa like her husband Mr. Oliver and her son, Edgar.

That night there was a special scent in their lovely house that God had blown there. Edgar remembered that night he was very hasty and he did everything immediately. He sat beside his father on a sofa downstairs and they pressed each other's hands firmly. They couldn't wait any longer. While waiting, his father told the story of Edgar's birthday to him. Listening to such a beautiful story at that time was enjoyable for Edgar.

Edgar was staring at upstairs. His mother's screams had surrounded the whole atmosphere of the home. Mr. Oliver had got very anxious for his poor wife. He loved her a lot and he couldn't tolerate her suffering.

Suddenly, screams evanished and it changed to crying. But a different kind of cry! It wasn't any adult person's cry. A kind of cry that was million times sweeter, happier, and warmer than any laugh in the world. It was Lisa's cry who greeted the new world. She put her first step in the road of life.

The door's lock opened and Mrs. Bennett came out. Mrs. Bennett was an old woman that helped pregnant women to deliver their child with traditional methods and she was very professional in her job. She was the best midwife in the area. She came out while she had taken Lisa inverted and hitting on her buttocks. Mr. Oliver looked at Lisa and then burst into tears. A beautiful blonde girl with gray eyes was God's gift to them. She had a big brown Mother's mark on her left shoulder. Maybe it was the sign of good luck for her.

Mrs. Bennett rolled Lisa in a brown towel and gave the tiny baby to her mother. Mrs. Oliver took Lisa and kissed her as much as she could and hugged her firmly. Mr. Oliver entered the room and sat beside them. He started looking at his tiny beautiful child and kissed her.

That night none of them could sleep; because of happiness. Their family's shape had changed. From that night Edgar felt being older as he had a younger sister now. He would never forget that moment although he grew older.

Edgar still dreamed of Lisa's birthday. A beautiful smile had sat on his lips. Suddenly, Mr. White hindered his dreams and called him to carry goods of one of the costumers. He stood up immediately and went inside. Since Edgar came to Mr. White's supermarket, his business had been become well and he could give better services to customers. He had hired many shop-boys in his supermarket before Edgar, but none of them made him satisfied and also unfortunately, some of them were light fingered. None of them could be as safe and polite as Edgar.

Edgar tied the stone inside a piece of cloth and put it in his pocket. He was very careful about it. That worthless stone valued for him more than everything else.

Chapter 2

Days passed one after the other. Passing time, some of Edgar's contemporaries in village found him very polite, kind, and loyal. They tried to be friends with him and get closer to him and his private life. They all could always see a sweet smile on his lips, but a deep sadness in his beautiful eyes. His behaviors were strange to them. He was not happy like other children.

Edgar was very handsome, personable, and tall and he seemed to be more than ten years old. He had blond hair like growing wheat in summer, blue eyes as like as the sky; masculine face with small and regular nose upon his scarlet lips. Behind all this external beauties, he had a big and kind heart that was pumping for tiny Lisa.

One day when he was sitting in front of the supermarket, he saw three boys coming to him. They were Bob, Teddy, and David. They were three close friends and had known each other for a long time.

Bob was the oldest among the three. He was eleven years old, and Teddy and David were ten. Bob was the only child of his family, and so, he had all his parents' attention on himself. His father was a farmer. They wished Bob be a teacher and teach in their own village. They did all their best to support his learning.

Teddy had two older sisters and he worked in his father's carpentry shop. He loved working with woods and he worked with all his heart. He was neither too silent nor too noisy.

David was the bravest boy in this group. He always loved danger and he didn't fear anything except his father's horrible shouts. His father, Mr. Robinson, was always drunk and coach-potato in front of the TV.

Their family's presidency was with his mother. She worked in spinning factory near the village and they got by with her salary. David's father hit him by his fist very often. He was really cruel and led-captain.

They got closer to Edgar and looked at him. Then they started greeting him.

"Where are you from, boy?" asked David.

Edgar was silent and he didn't say anything. He was just looking at them.

"Where is your home? Are you new here?" asked Teddy.

"We are your friends. We want to help you. You can trust us." said Bob in a kind voice.

Edgar was still silent and he looked at them. He had a bad experience of boys of the village when he bought the stone from those stupid boys. But this time he saw that these three boys are different. Finally, he started speaking to them and explained everything. Then he silenced again. Hearing Edgar's adventure, they got very sorry for him and started asking other questions from him.

"So, where is your sister now?" asked Bob.

"I don't know. I have looked everywhere that I could, but I didn't find her. I don't know what had really happened to her." answered Edgar in a small voice.

"It's too bad! But … but don't worry. You can count on us, buddy. We will help you find your sister as soon as possible. You can trust us. You are not alone any more. If we look for her together, we would find her sooner." said David pushing Edgar's hand.

"He is right! Don't worry. You'll see that we will find your sister very soon. I promise." continued Bob.

"Thank you my friends. I have really missed my sister. You know, I don't have anyone except her in my life. I can't believe she isn't beside me. And I can't think where she is and what she is doing now. I dream her every night." replied Edgar.

"She can't be far away. I have never had any younger sister, but I understand what you say. We know the village very well and we can look for her all places." said Teddy.

While they were speaking with each other, Mr. White called Edgar to help him in the supermarket.

"I have to go, my friends. Thanks coming. I feel better now because of having friends like you. See you latter." said Edgar and left them.

Bob, Teddy, and David left there and decided to go to their usual nest. Their nest was on a hill in the north part of the village and they could see the whole village from there. It was really an especial place.

They started to run as usual because the last one must get something for others the following time. It was a kind of wagering. They ran and ran, and finally when they reached the top of the hill, the last one was Bob. They were all panting. Every one lay in a side and they couldn't say even one word. Teddy and David were laughing at Bob because he had been the loser as usual.

A mild, chilly wind was blowing through the hill. Then some dark clouds came and darkened the sky. It seemed that it was about to rain. They rested for some minutes, then gathered beside each other and started speaking about Edgar and his poor sister. They were all felt pity for him. There was not the usual slyness in their faces.

"You see that? He was really worried about his sister and also sad because of his parent's death." said Teddy.

"You're right, Ted. He wasn't in a good mood. I think we've to help him find his sister as soon as possible. If he reaches his sister, he would be very happy…" said Bob.

"Yes! And if he found his sister, he would perhaps forget his parent's death. But … But how? How can we find Lisa? How can a 4-years-old child be alive all this time?" said David in a loud voice.

"I don't know how, boys! But we should help him. We can be beside him. In this way, he wouldn't feel alone and this is our first and best help to him now!" replied Bob.

"Of course, Bob! What do you think about taking him with us to fishing tomorrow? At least, he could forget everything for a day and have fun with us." said Teddy ambitiously.

"Wonderful! I LOVE FISHING. I promise Edgar will love, too. He will be very happy with this. Fortunately, you said a right word for the first time in your life, Ted." answered David happily and laughed at Teddy.

"Come on, boys! It's enough. Stop joking. It is going to rain. I feel some drops on my head. Let's go home before getting wet. I don't like to be drenched." said Bob and stood up.

They stood up immediately and started running toward their homes. Violent thunders cracked and made Teddy frightened, but David was laughing as loud as he could. He was so brave not to scare from thunders. They were running as fast as they could, but it wasn't useful and poor boys all got completely wet.

Next morning, Edgar was working in the shop as usual. He carried what Mr. White had bought from city. While he was raising a box he heard a voice that was calling him "Edgar … Edgar."

He turned around and saw David and Bob standing at the corner. He left the box on the ground and got closer to them.

"Hi. What are you doing here?" asked Edgar.

"Good morning, Edgar. We have good news for you. I'm sure you will be happy hearing it." said David.

"What is that? Is it about Lisa?" asked Edgar eagerly and hopefully. He looked forward to their news impatiently.

"Unfortunately, not …, but Ted, David, and I are going fishing today. We go fishing sometimes. Would you love to join us? You will enjoy it." smiled Bob.

"You confused me! I have never gone fishing before. I don't know how to fish. I would love to join you. That sounds like fun. But unfortunately I can't, my friends!" replied Edgar sadly.

"Why? What is wrong with it? What is the problem if you love to come?" asked David.

"You know, I'm working here and I have to work until evening. I don't think Mr. White would let me join you today. Maybe next time, my dear friends." answered Edgar.

"Come on, boy! That is not problem; I'll solve it. I know how to speak to Mr. White." said David and laughed. They laughed all together.

David took Edgar's hand and they went inside together. Mr. White was counting money with a smile on his lips. It seemed he had got a lot of money and he was in a good mood. And it was the best time for them to offer their request!

"Hi Mr. White, Good morning." said David in a small voice.

"Hi, David. Do you need anything?" answered Mr. White while counting money and didn't look at them.

"I don't need anything. I just have a request." said David.

"What is that?" answered Mr. White. He was still counting money and he didn't look at boys.

"I want to say… Bob, Teddy, and I are going fishing today! Would you let Edgar join us? I promise we will come back very soon and we will take care of him." said David and spoke like the most polite boy in the world. It was not believed that he was the usual naughty David. It seemed he knew his role very well.

Suddenly, Mr. White stopped counting money, lifted his head, and looked at Edgar in a strange way. He was silent and it made the boys fear. With his facial expression, Edgar thought that he won't let him join his friends. He put the money in the cash box, stood up from his chair and went toward the boys. They were more and more frightened.

"Do you wish to join them, Edgar?" asked Mr. White.

Edgar stared at the floor, cleared his throat, and said agitatedly "Yes, but … but if you accept and let me. I mean I'll do everything that you say… but when they told me about fishing, I told I had to work here and I couldn't come. But David said that he would talk to you and now we are here. Mr. White, what you say is important and I will do that…"

It was obvious that Edgar was very afraid and he didn't know what he was saying. He didn't want to dissatisfy his boss in any rate.

"It's enough … No matter! You can go, but promise to come back before evening. Be careful boys. Don't leave each other." said Mr. White kindly and made the boys self-collected.

Edgar lifted his head and took a deep breath and became very happy. He thanked his boss and then they ran outside with David.

"What happened boys? Did he accept?" asked Bob.

"Sorry to say, not. Edgar cannot join us." said David this and played the role of a sad person. But Edgar was laughing slowly and he couldn't play the role.

"Too bad. why?" asked Bob soft headedly.

"Come on, boy! How simple you are! He is happy, he is laughing, so what could have happened?" said David and continued, "Of course, yes! He is a very kind person unlike his gruff mien. He accepted without any problems. But we have to come back before evening."

"Wow! Excellent! Everything is going to be okay. Let's go and take Teddy." said Bob.

"Where is he?" asked Edgar.

"He is at home waiting for us. I think we have made late, he would be angry again like always. He is a wrathful boy." said David and laughed.

They all laughed and walked toward Teddy's place. His home was on the path. Their friendship was getting warmer and better and they were as close as friends for years. All these were because of Edgar's flexible and kind behavior. And he owed this behavior to his father who was the teacher of all excellencies. And also his kind mother who was the mother of all kindnesses in the world. He was a good fruit of a good family.

Passing alleys, Bob and David were busy speaking to each other about their plans to have fun in the fishing. They were habited to speak too much and they never got tired of speaking. Edgar followed them. Suddenly, something strange took all his attention and he stopped right away and turned around. He felt that he heard Lisa's voice from one of the windows. He got closer to that house, but he couldn't hear anything anymore! He just remembered that it was about one of the houses that he had carried goods for a woman last week.

He thought "It was a hallucination."

"Hey … Edgar! Why are you standing there? We are late! Come on, boy." shouted David.

A strong feeling was halting him in front of that window and he couldn't leave there easily. He could feel Lisa with all his heart and soul. "I must have been fancier" thought Edgar again and got sorry. He couldn't keep his friends waiting anymore, so he left there and joined them. He didn't say anything to his friends about it. He thought that it was just a sweet dream. A kind of sweet dream that he experienced many times. The more he thought about Lisa, the more he dreamed of her.

Teddy's house was at one end of the village and a bit far from center. He always had to walk this distance with his father to their carpentry shop in the center. His father and he were like friends of the same age and they had a very good friendship, so Teddy never felt alone even when he was far from his friends. And also he had two older sisters; twenty-year-old Linda and fourteen-year-old Rose that loved him a lot. They always wove colorful clothes for him. His oldest sister Linda was going to marry her love, Jack, in a few days.

When they reached Teddy, he was in front of their house and had a big fish-hook in his hand with a bottle of wet flies. It seemed that he had been waiting for a long time for his friends.

"Hey boys … I've been waiting for you for more than half an hour! Where were you at this time?" said Teddy a bit angrily, but not too much seriously.

"Nowhere. We were just getting Edgar's permission, so we came a little late!" answered David and smiled.

"Okay! No problem. It's your usual habit David. Let's go and enjoy ourselves." replied Teddy.

"Let's paint the town red" said Bob.

They walked through the forest to reach the fishing place that was beyond it. The forest was in the utter silence and there wasn't any sound of any creatures, except the sound of the boys' feet. After a while, the sound of water could be heard. They got closer to the river. The fishing place was not too far away, just about half an hour.

The forest was full of tall cypresses that divided sunlight to thousands of parts in the early morning. And also there were lots of fig-trees along the way they passed.

They were walking two by two, Edgar with Teddy, and Bob along with David in the front. David started joking with Bob as usual and they started beating and running after each other. They never could walk calmly. It was David who did not let.

In the back, Teddy was doing his best to take Edgar out from thinking about all bad events that had happened to him recently and make him laugh. He spoke to him a lot. He was trying to make him happy and laugh by telling jokes, interesting stories and news. But Edgar was calm, yet, and just was putting one foot in front of the other. But they spoke about their wishes and what they wanted to be in the future. Teddy insisted on continuing his father's occupation. When they were passing through the woods, he named the names of the all the trees. He knew them very well.

On the other side, Bob wanted to be a teacher and so do his parents. He mostly spoke about history and geography. He could be a very kind and sharp teacher. But David still thought about having fun and he never thought about future.

They walked and walked; finally, reached a silent place. There wasn't any sound heard, except birds singing and water's footfall. There was a wide river with clear water and the stones in the water were seen easily. Even the small frogs were seen, which were like small fishes because their legs and hands hadn't grown yet.

Edgar was completely surprised at seeing such a fantastic view in front of him. The shadow of the trees on the water had made a dreamful scene. Tall green reeds had surrounded the river and some lilies were found among them. Everything was ready for having a day full of joy.

David took out his shoes rapidly and put his feet in the cold water then he started singing loudly. Unluckily, his voice was like an angry lion that was hungry and wanted to eat something, but unfortunately, his friends had to bear it.

Teddy started making his fish-hook ready to catch the poor fish. Fish whose final day had come and could not escape their destiny. He was putting wet flies on top of the hook to deceive the hungry fish. Exactly the time that the poor fish wanted to eat food, became food for others. And it is nature and nobody could do anything.

Teddy sat on a big stone on the bank of the river and Edgar sat beside him interested in fishing. He wanted to learn how to fish. He was clever enough to pick up everything very soon. He looked at what Teddy was doing accurately.

Bob summoned David to go with him to collect fire woods to grill the hunted fish freshly. David took out his feet out of water, wore his shoes, and followed Bob while still singing. He never got tired of singing. Maybe he wanted to be a singer in the future. All around the river was full of fire woods and they didn't have to go far.

Teddy and Edgar were still waiting for a fish sitting beside river. There was a special curiosity in Edgar's eyes.

"Can I hold it, Teddy? I want to learn how to fish!" said Edgar with a lot of curious in his eyes.

"Of course, yes! You can try your chance. Hold the hook firmly. When you felt it is shaking, take it out rapidly. But be careful not to let the fish flee. They are very nimble animals." said Teddy and explained all he knew about fishing.

"Thanks … I'll do my best!" replied Edgar and laughed. He took the fish-hook from him and started waiting for fish. He clenched the hook firmly and was serious to catch a fish to show his abilities to his friends. He waited for a while, but there was no sign of any fish.

On the other side, Bob and David were making a fire. They collected a large quantity of fire woods as they wanted to grill all the fish in the river, but poor boys didn't know their friends hadn't caught any fish even one. David was blowing on fire and his face was turned to black. He was crazy about doing such things. Playing with fire was a joy for him.

Suddenly, they all heard Edgar's voice that was shouting "Fish … Fish … Fish, I have caught a big one… my hook is heavy …"

They forgathered around him and helped him to take out the hook from water. When the hook came out of the water they all started laughing loudly and every one lay in a side. David was about to die of laughter. Edgar first got sorry for his chance, but then he started laughing too because he had caught a big watery tin. But he didn't despair and threw his hook in the water again. He started waiting for a fish again and his friends went around their fire and got busy with that.

Their fire was getting stronger and stronger, but unfortunately, there was no fish to grill in it. Poor boys could do nothing except just listening to David's singing.

After a short time, Edgar again felt something in his hook, but he didn't tell his friends this time and tried to take it out slowly. When he took out the hook a big smile sat on his face because there was a white big salmon on top of the hook that was shining like a diamond.

"Hey, boys! Look. Edgar has caught a fish." shouted David and ran toward Edgar.

"Bravo ...Bravo, Edgar." said Teddy happily. "You are an excellent fisher."

They all forgathered around him again and helped him to free the fish from the hook. Now they had something to grill on the fire and eat. David took the fish from them and ran to fire. He immediately put the fish on a poke and made it ready to grill.

While they were happy and laughing, a sudden accident changed their beautiful day. They were leaving the river and coming to the fire through the bank of it. Edgar slipped on a stone and he fell in the river. The middle of the river was very fast and hard. Teddy tried to take his hands, but it was too late and Edgar was going down through the river. His friends followed him along the river, shouting his name. David saw them and left the fish on the ground and ran toward them as fast as he could. He saw an old broken tree that had crossed the river a bit further down. It was the only chance that they could reach Edgar. So, David increased his speed to reach there before Edgar. He was steeped in perspiration. He was running with all his might while Teddy and Bob were running behind him.

"David ... Bob ...." Edgar was screaming and calling his friends to save him.

"I am here, boy! I'll save you, Edgar ... just resist ... I'll save you ... I promise ..." shouted David loudly while there were some small tears in his eyes. His feet had grown numb as he was running so fast.

David reached that broken tree and lay on it immediately; then stretched his hands to the water. Bob and Teddy were holding David from his feet. Edgar was getting closer. David stretched his hand again as long as he could and when Edgar reached there, he took his hands by top of his fingers. Then he tried to pull him out, but it was too hard because Edgar was wet and heavier, and his hands were slimy. None the less, he did his best and took out Edgar from the water; then lay him down on the grass with Bob and Teddy's help.

Edgar had become very weak. He couldn't speak too much and just he was pointing on his right shin. They tore his pants immediately. He had injured his shin terribly with a big wound. Edgar was suffering the wound and couldn't move his leg.

All the boys were shocked and they didn't know what to do. In the interim, Teddy stood up and ran toward forest and vanished for a while. David and Bob couldn't find out what he wanted to do. After minutes, he came back with two big woods in his hands.

"We have to make stretcher to carry him to village. He can't walk with us. He should not shake his leg." said Teddy hurriedly.

"Okay ... but how?" asked Bob.

"I'll say. Just take out your coats" replied Teddy.

They took out their coats, tied them to each other, and made a big piece of cloth. Then they tied the cloth to the woods and made a comfortable stretcher for their friend. Edgar was still suffering and was getting worse moment after moment.

David took out his shirt, too and tied Edgar's wound firmly. Then they laid Edgar on the stretcher. They were all worried about their friend. They were ready to do everything for their dear friend.

Teddy went to the bank of the river, packed his bag and took the fish Edgar had hunted immediately. Then he put out the fire and came back to his friends. Then they started walking toward the village while Bob and David were carrying Edgar on their shoulders.

"How shall we tell Mr. White about Edgar?" asked David worriedly.

"I don't know, but I'm sure he would be very angry with us!" said Bob.

"I'm sure he would kill us..." said Teddy in a small voice.

"It has happened and we can't do anything. Now, we have to take Edgar to the doctor, immediately. He has lost a lot of blood." said Bob.

"Yes. I do agree with you. But first let's take him to Mr. White and then call Doctor Paul!" replied Teddy.

"We deserve what Mr. White would tell us..." said David.

They increased their speed and walked faster and faster.

It was about noon and the weather was getting warmer. As they were getting closer to the village they were getting more anxious because of thinking about Mr. White's reaction to this event. Passing time, Edgar was getting weaker and he was just murmuring some things in a very small and vague voice that nobody could understand what exactly he was saying.

When they entered the village, everybody was looking at them strangely. But the boys didn't pay attention to them and walked straightly toward the supermarket. Mr. White was in front of the supermarket busy with fruit. They went closer and laid down the stretcher behind Mr. White, but none of them dared to say anything. They just stared at ground and stood beside the stretcher. While Mr. White was sibilating, turned around and saw the scene. He didn't believe what he was seeing and was completely shocked. He closed and opened his eyes several times and finally stared at the stretcher. Then he raised up his head and looked at the boys angrily while his skin had been turned to red. The boys were just looking down at their toes. None of them dared to say any word. They were all ashamed.

"What has happened to Edgar? What is this hell? Why is he on the stretcher? Why is his leg bloody?" stormed Mr. White loudly and looked angrily at the boys.

David cleared his throat and said in a very very small voice, "He ... He was fishing and suddenly he ..."

But Mr. White cut in on his voice and shouted again, "shut your mouth! And call Doctor Paul, immediately. Help me take him in."

"What happened to you, poor boy" said Mr. White slowly while he was looking at Edgar's bloody leg.

David left there soon to call doctor. Bob and Teddy raised up the stretcher and took it in. Mr. White brought a wet cloth and cleaned the blood from Edgar's body and gave him a glass of juice to keep him strong. He was very worried. He liked Edgar as if he is his own son. It was hard for him to see Edgar in that situation.

After a quarter, Doctor Paul and David arrived. David was panting as he had run all the way to save his friend sooner. Doctor sat beside the stretcher looking at Edgar's wound and opened his bag and took out his equipment and started his work. He opened the wound and looked at it.

"How is it going, doctor?" asked Mr. White worriedly.

"He has been injured very hard. There is a fracture in his bone. He can't walk for a long time." said Doctor sadly still looking at Edgar's leg.

"Doctor Paul? Can you say exactly how long?" Asked Bob.

"I think at least about four months. He has to rest this time." answered Doctor.

"After that time, would he be able to walk as usual?" asked Mr. White worriedly.

"I hope yes. But everything depends on him. Now let me bandage his leg with splints." said Doctor and started making materials to bandage Edgar's broken leg.

All the boys and Mr. White got sorry for poor Edgar hearing the bad news from the doctor. Mr. White again looked at the boys seriously as he wanted to kill them. Doctor took out stitching equipment from his bag and started to put stitches in Edgar's wound. Then he bandaged his leg with splints and gave some drug to Mr. White with instructions of them.

"Do not move his leg in any case, at least for some weeks. It has been fractured terribly. And give these drug to him daily. I have written instructions on them. He would be conscious completely tomorrow. Just let him sleep today. Occurring any problem, call me soon." said Doctor, collected his equipment in his bag, and left the supermarket.

Mr. White went out speaking with doctor and after while came back in to the supermarket. The boys were still standing beside Edgar and all of them were very sad and also scared. They were completely silent as they didn't have anything to say because they had promised Mr. White to take care of Edgar, but now they had failed to do that and they were ready for any punishment. Mr. White stood beside them. All of them held down their head and kept silent.

"You boys! You promised me to take care of him? But now you have brought him on a stretcher with a broken a leg?" shouted Mr. White at them.

"We … we are sorry. We were all happy catching a fish then suddenly he fell down in the river and …" answered Bob in a very small voice.

"Keep still…! I don't want to hear anything anymore. I can't keep him here now. I have to take him home. You three … take him out. Wait for me to close the supermarket and then help me take him home." said Mr. White.

"Yes, sir…" said Teddy.

"Surely, Mr. White…" said David.

Edgar was completely unconscious now. They took him out of the supermarket and waited for Mr. White to close the shop. Then he came and they started to walk toward his home while Teddy and David were carrying Edgar on the Stretcher. The home wasn't too far, just three allies away.

Mr. White had a very kind wife and a 9-year-old daughter. He had spoken about Edgar to his family before, but he had never taken him to his house, so his wife was eager to see Edgar, but surly not in that bad condition.

They reached home and, Mr. White knocked at the door. After a while, his wife came and opened the door. By the moment she opened the door, she got surprised facing that scene. She didn't say anything and just stood a side. The boys carried Edgar inside. Then they took him to one of the rooms in the upstairs. They left there soon. Mary went beside Mr. White and looked at injured boy.

"I think he must be Edgar. But why so?" asked Mary.

“You are right. This is Edgar; the boy I had spoken about before. In the morning his friends came and asked me to take him to fishing with them. When I felt that Edgar desired to go, I didn’t deny. But when they come back, everything was like you see now…” answered Mr. White and took out his hat, put in a corner, and scratched his head.

“Take it easy! We will take care of him. I always loved to have a son. Sara and I will take care of him and he can be a good friend for Sara at home.” smiled Mary.

“Thanks Mary! You have always helped me in hard situations. Um ... you said Sara … Where is my honey, now?” asked Mr. White.

“She is taking bath. It has been a long time. Let me get her.” replied Mary.

Mary went toward the bathroom. When she reached there, Sara was drying herself. She was really pretty and gorgeous. She had long blonde hair with green eyes and she was tall. When she came out, her mother told her about the guest. Sara got very happy hearing the news, and asked her mother about the guest. Mary explained everything to him.

Sara felt pity for poor Edgar and asked Mary to go and visit him. Her mother agreed and they went to Edgar’s room together. They opened the door slowly and entered the room. The room which used to be vacant for a long time. Mr. White had left the room to bring water and pills for Edgar.

Edgar was still unconscious and asleep on the bed. Sara got closer and closer, and looked at Edgar for a long time. When she saw him in that condition, her eyes burst into tears. In this time, his father came holding a tray on his hands. He had brought Edgar’s drug with a glass of water. He raised his head and put a pill in his mouth and helped him to swallow it. Edgar was still semiconscious and his mouth’s muscles were working hard.

“Oh, I see my darling daughter is here.” said Mr. White and sat beside the bed. “He would get better with these drugs and tomorrow he will be completely conscious. Now he just needs to rest. My dear Sara, Let’s leave him alone…” said Mr. White.

Sara kissed his father and went to her room. It was beside Edgar's room. She stayed in the bed thinking about Edgar. During the night, when her parents were asleep, she couldn't halt herself and went to Edgar's room and visited him twice, but he was asleep. The bright moon had lightened the room. She took another look at Edgar and went back to her room.

Now she was very happy because of having a friend in the house and she didn't feel alone any longer. That night, she looked at the stars in the sky from her room's window and spoke to them. Stars were her friends all her lonely nights. But that night, she told to stars that she had a new friend who was sleeping in the next room. While she was speaking to stars she fell asleep.

Next morning, a shiny sun was shining in the sky of the village. Sparrows were singing loudly in the garden and the flowers were getting up. Sky was as blue as a sea and there was no sign of any cloud. Chicks were following their mother in the yard.

Mr. White woke up and when he got out of his room, he saw his wife making breakfast in the kitchen. As usual, she decorated the table with fresh flowers and delicious food.

"Good morning, my good soul…" said Mary.

"Good morning, Mary. You are looking prettier than always. Let me go and visit Edgar." replied Mr. White.

He went upstairs and entered Edgar's room. He was still asleep. He got closer to him and sat beside his bed. Then he called Edgar slowly. He didn't wake up and Mr. White called him some more times. Finally, he opened his eyes and moved his head slowly on the pillow. He stared at Mr. White and he was surprised that where he is. He tried to move in the bed, but he couldn't and his leg ached painfully.

"Don't move, Edgar. You have been terribly injured. You have to rest a long time." said Mr. White.

"Where …where am I, now?" asked Edgar in a small voice.

"You are in my home. My family will take care of you here, till you get better." answered Mr. White.

"But … but I can't stay here … I have to work in your supermarket… I can't rest in your home." said Edgar and tried to move from his bed again, but he couldn't and made a loud scream.

"Look … you couldn't move, boy. You have been injured. You will work beside me in the supermarket after you get well." answered Mr. White.

"But I am a shop-boy. I have to work?" said Edgar looking at Mr. White.

"You needn't do anything. You were a great shop-boy for me all this time, and I like to help you any time. You will work there after you get better. After breakfast, I will introduce my family to you. And now, just take a rest and don't try to shake your leg." replied Mr. White.

"Thank you, sir … you are very kind." said Edgar.

Mr. White left Edgar's room and went toward his daughter's room. When he entered, he saw that Sara is rolling on his bed. He went closer and made a big kiss on Sara's cheek and hugged her firmly. Then they went downstairs to eat breakfast. Mary was waiting for them in the kitchen with a beautiful decorated table.

Sara loved carrot jam a lot. Her mother always had to bring carrot jam for her. They all had a big breakfast and after that Mr. White asked them to go with him to Edgar' room. Mary brought a big breakfast on a tray for the sick boy. They went inside and stood beside the bed and Mr. White started to introduce his family to Edgar.

"This is my wife, Mary. You can ask him whatever you need." said Mr. White.

"Hi, Edgar … Welcome to our home." said Mary.

"Hi." replied Edgar in a small voice.

"And this is my lovely daughter, Sara. She would be your friend." said Mr. White hugging Sara.

"Hi, Edgar. You are quite welcome" said Sara staring at Edgar's eyes.

"Hi, Sara. I have to thank all of you. You are very kind." replied Edgar with a sweet smile on his lips.

"Now everybody, I have to go. Good bye, Mary. Take care of children."

Mr. White said this and went off toward supermarket. He was a bit sad because he didn't have his shop-boy now.

Mary went downstairs and left Edgar and Sara alone in the room.

Sara was too happy because she felt that she had an older brother now and she didn't feel alone anymore.

Sara was a painter and she had drawn beautiful pictures. She went to her room and came back with three of her pictures and showed all of them to Edgar. Edgar was surprised at Sara's talent because her pictures were really beautiful. Then Sara started to speak about whatever came to her mind. About her friends, her family, her school, her interests, and whatever passed her mind. That moment, Edgar was completely silent with a smile on his lips. He listened to her carefully. Suddenly, Edgar started to cough and he asked Sara to bring water for him. Sara went to her mother and fetched a glass of water rapidly.

"Now, Edgar … it's your turn to speak about yourself. I spoke for a long time, and now, I want to hear you" said Sara.

"I … I don't have anything to say, but I have to confess you spoke very well and I enjoyed." replied Edgar.

"You can speak about your family or your friends. I like to hear." insisted Sara.

When Sara asked Edgar to speak about his family, he got sad and stared at an old tree out of the window.

"Did I bother you asking about your family?" asked Sara.

"I don't have any family … I lost them in a terrible accident. I don't have a sweet adventure like yours. And nothing enjoyable to say. Of course, I had a very good family in which everybody loved each other. My mother, Venus, was the goddess of kindness. I had a brave father that was a big secure support in my life. And finally my tiny sister, Lisa, was the sweetness of our family. Everything was going well till a horrible accident destroyed all my family and also my life. Now, I think I'm just following the destiny. I have to go wherever it guides me." said Edgar in a very small and sad voice and then he explained everything to Sara.

Sara was shocked about Edgar's destiny and again felt pity for him. Her eyes burst into tears again, but she didn't let herself cry beside him. In that moment, a wild pigeon alighted behind the window and started signing loudly, but sadly. The ambience of room became romantic and silence was the king of that.

Both Sara and Edgar were looking at each other's eyes without saying a word. They spoke with their eyes because no word in the world could explain whatever passing in their mind. None of the colors in the world could draw that scene. Two innocent looks crossed each other in the beautiful ambience of the room.

Sara took Edgar's hand firmly and then said to him, "you need to rest; I won't bother you any more, I'll come back soon to visit you again." Then she left him and went to her mother. She was knitting a jacket for Sara in red. Sara sat beside her chair and put her head on her mother's knees. Mary put her knitting needle away and combed Sara's hair by her fingers. Her fingers were like a wind crossing through the woods. Then they started speaking about Edgar and his fate.

"Mom! Edgar has lost all his family; it is very poignant, isn't it?" asked Sara.

"Yes, my darling. He is in a bad condition. The worst of all, he lost his sister, too. He is still tenacious to find her, but I am not sanguine. How can a 4-year-old girl be alive among this long time!" replied Mary.

"I really got sorry for him. I can't imagine living without you even for one day, Mom! Never leave me alone. I love you, Mom." said Sara and kissed her mother.

"I, too, love you my dear daughter. You are all my life. Your dad and I do everything for you and your future. You are the success of our love." replied Mary and smiled.

After about two hours the door bell rang. Mary opened the door and saw Bob, Teddy, and David. They had come to visit their friend. They entered home having a big fish in their hands. It was the fish that Edgar had hunted previous day. They gave it to Mary and she guided them upstairs to Edgar's room.

When they entered the room, she left the boys alone and went down. Edgar got very jolly seeing his friends. They surrounded Edgar's bed and all started speaking to him.

"How are you, fisher man?" said David and laughed.

"I'm in good health, my friends. Mr. White and his family are really kind people and they prepare everything I need. I don't know how to thank them." replied Edgar.

"We know how! We have brought the fish that you hunted yesterday. You were excellent in fishing. It is very big. Mr. White's family and you can eat it all together. They will enjoy it." said Teddy.

"Really! I hunted a fish, but instead I broke my leg." said Edgar and smiled.

"Take it easy, boy. You will walk very soon. The important thing is that you have hunted such a big fish that we have never hunted before. And never forget this; who wants to succeed must pass drudgeries. You know, no pains no gains." said Bob.

"Come on, boys. It was just chance…" replied Edgar.

"Chance or whatever it was, you were great. How are you feeling now? Are you still in pain?" asked Bob.

"I'm fine, but … but I'm suffering something else." said Edgar this with a lot of sorrow.

"What is wrong with you, boy?" asked Teddy curiously.

"Mr. White said that I have to rest for about four months or perhaps more. In this case, I can't go outside and it means that I can't look for Lisa this long time. I don't know what she is doing now and where she is. I don't know what may have happened to her. I can't resist her absence anymore. I have really missed her." said Edgar this and his eyes burst into tears.

The ambience of room changed from glee to gloom. All of them got silent, but David broke silence and said, "Don't worry, Edgar. We will look for her every possible place. Lisa is not just your sister; she is our sister, too. We love her as much as you do, and we will do our best to find her. And now just give a big smile to us; we don't crave to see you cheerless anytime."

"Thank you, boys. Your presence is a secure support for me. I lost my family, but instead, I have found good friends like you and also Mr. White and his kind family." replied Edgar.

"Edgar, would you tell us more about your sister?" asked Teddy.

"Of course, she is a blonde girl with gray eyes. She has a necklace the same as mine. You can see it on my neck. They are fully alike. It should be on her neck if nobody has robbed it from her, so far." answered Edgar.

"Be sure we will look for her. Now, we have to go before Mr. White's arrival. You know, he is very angry with us. We couldn't keep our promise and take care of you. He is right to be angry with us." said Bob.

"You are not guilty. I slipped myself. All in all, thanks for coming." said Edgar.

"We are always with you." said David.

"Good bye, fisher man." said Teddy.

"We will come again. Bye Edgar." said Bob.

They left Edgar and again he remained in his solitude with a broken and bandaged leg. He ate some of his drug and then slept.

The days were passing one after another and there were no sign of Edgar's sister. His friends came and visited him two or three times a week, but each time, without any news of Lisa. Along this time, Edgar and Sara's friendship were getting closer and closer. They always sat with each other and spoke for a long time about everything that made them busy.

After about one week, Sara started to teach Edgar painting or any other hobbies that she knew. Sara's presence helped Edgar to feel Lisa's absence less and less and mutually Sara didn't feel alone at home anymore since Edgar came. Edgar was extremely clever as he could learn painting very soon, and it made Sara surprised.

The walls of the room were covered with beautiful pictures that they had drawn. Edgar's first skilled painting was about a volcano eruption scene. But he drew to red hearts in the picture instead of his parents. And also a beautiful flower that was Lisa.

Chapter 3

Five months later

Everywhere was covered by red, yellow and orange leaves that had fallen down from trees. The trees had been bare. The wind was moving leaves from one side to another side on the soil. They had to move wherever wind led them. They were not heavy enough to resist before wind. The weather was colder than before. Small white rabbits were fallowing each other in leaves. It seemed they liked the sound which produced by breaking leaves under their feet. Swallows were singing the song of autumn on the bare branches of the trees. Everywhere was a beautiful picture of an autumn.

It was about one o'clock at noon. Fallen leaves were scrunching and making noise under the feet of a girl. It was Sara. She was coming back from school. She was walking very slowly toward home as she was very tired after spending a tiring day at school. When she reached the fences of their home, she looked inside and saw a surprising scene. She saw Edgar walking in the yard with her mother. She didn't believe that Edgar walking without any walking sticks or her mother's assist.

She ran toward them and called Edgar loudly. Edgar and Mary turned back and saw Sara coming. Edgar got surprised, too, and fell down. They all laughed. It was a beautiful day for all of them.

"Edgar … you are walking … I'm really joyful to see you walking." said Sara loudly.

"Right… I owe everything to you and your family. You took a lot of pains to take care of me." replied Edgar.

“There was no pain. You’re like my own son, and I love you as much as I do Sara.” said Mary.

Mary took their hands and they went inside together. They went to kitchen and sat around the lunch table and waited for Mr. White to come back from work. After about half an hour, he came and Mary opened the door, but she didn’t say anything about Edgar’s walking.

While Mr. White was taking out his coat, he saw Edgar walking toward him. He got very surprised and went closer and hugged Edgar firmly. It was a beautiful scene. After Edgar, Sara came and hugged his father. Now, Edgar was on the left and Sara on the right, as if both of them were Mr. White’s own children. Still in his bosom, they went to kitchen to eat lunch.

Mary was a great cook. Nobody could wait for lunch even for a second. They sat around the lunch table and prayed before eating. In the last sentences of the pray, they all thanked God for Edgar’s health. Then, they began to eat delicious foods before them. After first spoon, Mr. White started to praise Mary’s tasty foods as usual.

“Believe me; no one could cook like you. You are the best.” said Mr. White and ate his delicious lunch hurriedly.

After lunch Sara and his mother got busy cleaning the table and washing the dishes. Mr. White and Edgar went out of kitchen and sat on a sofa. Mr. White told to Edgar that he could work in the supermarket beside him again.

Edgar got happy hearing that because he wanted to requite all their kindnesses by working hard in the supermarket. He went out to walk lonely in the yard. After staying on bed for month, he was avid to walk.

Edgar was an appreciative boy and he knew that if there were not any Mr. White, what disasters would happen to him and what calamities he would face! He knew that he owed all his life to him and his family. The most important was Sara’s presence which lightened the lack of Lisa. He was disappointed to find his sister after this long time. He was disappointed to reach her again, to look at her beautiful eyes, to kiss her cheeks, and hug her firmly.

He took out the stone that he had bought for Lisa's birthday. He looked at it for a while and wanted to throw it away, but he changed his mind and put it in his pocket again.

He had believed that he had to continue the rest of his life alone without any members of his family. Life seemed very cruel and savage in front of his eyes. He thought that what would happen to the world if his family were alive now; at least Lisa. He asked himself, "Were they extra in this big world?" But he calmed down when he remembered that all of these events were God's volition and no one could change it. He remembered that he has a God that would help him every time and everywhere.

He was putting one foot after another along allies while his mind was full of questions, wishes and dreams. The wind combed his hair kindly. He sat on a side and looked at leaves falling down from the trees. At the end of the alley, there was a school. When he saw the school, he missed the days he studied in. He was very clever and one of the best students of their school. But now he had to work and couldn't go to school to continue his studies. Lots of regrets and wishes had been drawn in his mind that moment. He tried to forget the past and just think about the future awaited him.

Now, he could feel that he is not a child any longer. He was grown. A young adult who did not have any family. A young adult who had to live a lonely life without his father's supports and his mother's kindnesses.

Lost deep in thoughts, he felt someone calling him from behind. He turned around and saw Teddy walking toward him. He was with his father and they were coming back from work. He left his father and walked toward Edgar. When Teddy saw Edgar walking, he got amazed and ran to him. He was very happy of seeing his friend healthy. They walked in the allies for a while and went home.

Next early morning, Edgar went to work with his boss. He was happy to be able to work there again. When he reached the supermarket, he cleaned everywhere and arranged all the shelves. When costumers came to shop and saw Edgar, all of them got happy. Edgar's good behavior caused all costumers love him.

Now, Mr. White was more comfortable because Edgar did most of the things and he just had to count money.

About the noon, when Edgar was on his way back to supermarket, he saw Bob and David coming back from school. He greeted them on the path and left them very soon to go back to the shop. When he reached, Mr. White was getting ready to go home for lunch. He asked Edgar to go with him to their home, but he didn't accept his offer and said that he would eat lunch in the shop like he used to. Mr. White left the supermarket and went home alone. When he reached home, Mary and Sara asked about Edgar. Mr. White said why he didn't accept himself to come with him.

"He is a very polite boy. I have missed him just this little while. I really love him. I wish I had a son like him." said Mary and sighed slowly.

"Not only polite, he is also very active. Today, I was more comfortable with his presence in the shop. I think he is God's gift for me…" said Mr. White.

"Dad, I have to say he is also very clever. He could learn painting very soon and now he paints even better than me. But I regret that he is not with us now and I feel alone at home again." Lisa said and went upstairs to her room.

Elsewhere, in the supermarket, Edgar was having lunch with only a chocolate cake, although his boss had allowed him to eat everything he liked in the shop. But he was satisfied with that small chocolate cake.

After finishing lunch, he cleaned all the shop. When Mr. White came back, he saw everywhere was clear. Seeing all these, he got more and more satisfied with him. That day, they had a lot of costumers and they worked late at night. Edgar was too tired as he had carried a lot of goods many times that evening, but he loved his work and fatigue didn't make him nervous. He worked with all his might and heart. He knew that he had to requite Mr. White and his family's kindnesses.

When Mr. White decided to go home, he asked Edgar to go with him, but Edgar didn't accept again. He was more comfortable in the shop. So, Mr. White went out and left Edgar alone in the supermarket. Edgar opened his blanket behind the refrigerator and put a small pillow under his head.

When he slept, he dreamed a big palace and many waitresses around him. He was bossing around. He was one of the richest people in the area. All the girls around him wished to marry him, but he desired none of them. He was very famous and everybody knew him very well. But suddenly, he woke up with a loud sound of a thunder. He got up and understood that everything was just a dream. Then he neared to the window and looked outside. It was raining heavily. Thunders crashed the dark sky. He could smell wet soil. It was very favorable. He looked outside for a while and then went back to his bed again and tried to sleep well as he had to work the following day.

Next morning, the opening locks woke Edgar up. He got up immediately and greeted his boss in the shop entrance. Mr. White entered, took out his coat and hanged it behind the chair, and then he said that he had good news.

"Tomorrow is Sara's birthday." He said this and collected some needed goods and gave them to Edgar.

"Take these things to home and help them to decorate the home for birthday." said Mr. White.

Edgar lifted all the bags rapidly and walked home. He was happy that he could meet Mary and Sara again. When Mary opened the door she got happy seeing Edgar and called Sara soon. Sara came downstairs and greeted Edgar warmly. Edgar congratulated her birthday. Then, they got busy decorating the home. Edgar was blowing balloons and Sara was writing names of guests that she wanted to invite for her birthday. Most of them were her school friends.

About noon, they finished decorating. When Mr. White came back to home, he liked their ornament and thanked Mary, Edgar, and Sara. Edgar was very pleased that day and he thought that he was beside his own family. He didn't feel alone anymore. He was forgetting all bad events that had happened to him before. He started new life beside a new family. He was getting older day by day and emotions in his life were giving their place to logic.

There was battle in his mind between past and future; present was the battlefield. He tried to forget his past completely and think about the future and success. He wanted to make a happy future to requite his gloomy past. He liked to be a big person and in that way, help other deprived people.

After lunch, Lisa and Edgar went out to spread invitation cards. They did it till evening and went back to home. That night, Sara's insistence kept Edgar with them. Next morning they got up early and checked everything again for the big party. Everything was okay, orderly, and ready to entertain the guests. Mr. White went to supermarket to leave children comfortable at home.

After some hours, the guests came one by one. After a while, the home was full of young girls and boys. Teddy and David were there, but not Bob because he had gone to city with his father.

Everybody started to dance, but Edgar didn't know how to dance because he had never been in such parties in their small village.

Sara introduced Edgar to all of her friends proudly. They all loved Edgar since he was very handsome and good-looking. The most importantly, he was too respectful and polite to everyone. All of them tried to dance with Edgar for a while and other boys envied him about this matter. On the other hand, Sara's friends envied her close friendship with Edgar. In one word, everybody in that party spoke about Sara and Edgar.

Finally, Mary came out of the kitchen holding a big birthday cake. It was very big and beautiful and it took everyone's attention in the party. Then Sara blew the candles and entered the tenth spring of her life. Everybody clapped her and asked her to dance with Edgar. Edgar got surprised and didn't know what to say or do. Sara took his hand and they started dancing together in the middle of a circle that the boys and girls had made. Sara was looking at Edgar's eyes in a very strange and lovely way that was completely different from a sister's look into a brother's eyes. Edgar got disturbed about this matter, left her hands, and sat on a sofa in a corner of room beside his friends, David and Teddy. Hi deed, made Sara bothered.

The party continued until evening. All were weary of dancing. They left the party one after the other. The last one was Edgar that wanted to go to the shop and sleep there. Sara insisted him to stay at home that night and sleep there, but he didn't accept and walked toward the supermarket. When he reached the shop Mr. White was closing the door.

"Don't close it sir, I am staying here." said Edgar.

"Edgar! You have come? How was the party? Did you enjoy?" asked Mr. White.

"It was very fine. I hadn't seen such a party before and it was enjoyable for me." answered Edgar.

"Okay! Nice dancing. Take care of yourself. See you tomorrow, boy." said Mr. White and left.

"Good bye, sir. Good night." replied Edgar.

Edgar was very tired, so he opened his blanket behind the refrigerator as usual and slept the moment he closed his eyes. His place was too small, but it was the most comfortable bed for him in the world. That night he dreamed about all events that had happened to him in the party. He was dancing with Sara in the middle of angels that had surrounded them on the clouds. Each angel was playing a kind of musical instruments. They were playing the tone of his life. Everything was romantic and full of emotions.

Next morning Mr. White came to the supermarket and unlocked the doors. He saw Edgar still sleeping deeply. He got surprised because he would always find him awake when he opened the door. But this time, he was asleep with a sweet smile on his lips. Mr. White woke him up and went behind his cash box and got busy counting money and other stuffs. Edgar got ashamed that he was asleep when his boss came. He got up rapidly and started his work in the supermarket with inflated eyes.

"I have to go to city and buy some needs. I will be back until noon. Take care of the supermarket till I come back." said Mr. White.

"Yes, sir. I will." answered Edgar.

Then Mr. White ignited his small old blue lorry and drove toward city. Edgar came back inside and decorated all the goods in the shop. It wasn't a busy day and he was free there. So, he started painting a picture with instruments that Sara had given to him before.

He drew a big garden with tall trees and colorful flowers. In the middle of picture, there was a girl and a boy who had stared at each other lovingly. They were speaking to each other through their eyes, living in a silent picture. They loved to move and reach each other, but they were just pictures, and couldn't move forward even a foot. They were pictures, and they had to be pictures forever. He drew a big shiny sun that was a gateway toward hope in his eyes. There was a blue river that was going to join the sea of his wishes in the future. There weren't any clouds in the sky of his picture, although he loved rain and drops a lot.

His progress in painting was very good and he had learned it very well; even he could paint better than Sara, now. It was his tenth picture that he had drawn. Each one was better than the previous. He hung his last picture on the wall of the shop behind Mr. White's table. When he turned back, he saw a tall pretty girl standing beyond the cash box. She had worn a beautiful scarlet dress. She was Teddy's sister; Rose. Edgar didn't know her because he hadn't seen her before, but Rose knew Edgar as Teddy had spoken about him to her. She wanted some sugar and eggs. While Edgar was making ready her needs he was looking at her furtively. She was very attractive and pretty. When he made her needs ready, she paid money and went out without saying any words, but a simple "thank you." She had some books in her hands. They reminded Edgar school periods. He was too sad that he couldn't study at school, but he wanted to transcend all his contemporaries. He wanted to be an important person in the society, in the future. He was full of wishes.

It was about noon, and the sound of the lorry could be heard nearing. Edgar went out and saw his boss coming. Rear of the small lorry was full of things. He started taking them off and then put them inside. Mr. White was very tired and he went inside and drank three cups of coffee. It wasn't useful and he tried the fourth and fifth. He was too thirsty as if he hadn't drunk coffee for months. He started complaining about city's pollution and crowd, as usual.

"I would never change my simple life in this village with a life in a city. They are eating pollution all day. Instead, I am in the middle of trees and nature, here. Everywhere is crowd and busy. The sound of bugles made me crazy. I wake up with sounds of singing birds every morning, but they wake up with sound of harsh cars. This is too much of a good thing, isn't it, Edgar?" said Mr. White.

"I don't know, sir. I have never been to a city. I don't know how they live." answered Edgar.

"I have news for you. Maybe you love and maybe you don't. Come and sit here." said Mr. White.

"Yes, sir… I listen." replied Edgar

"Today, when I was shopping in the city center, I saw one of my old friends. He was a friend of my childhood. We were neighbors. He left here with his family years ago and he has been living in the city ever since. But my parents stayed here. Now, both of us have grown old. He said that he is in computer business now and he has become very rich and strong. And also, wellbeing had made him very fat and obese; instead his childhoods that he was scrawny like a stood skeleton. All in all, he has become very successful in his life. Then he asked me if I had a son to send beside him to work in his company and grow in a city environment, not in a village. And I replied that I have just a daughter. But then I remembered you and I told him about you. I said that you're like my own child. Edgar? Would you like to go there, live in the city, and work in a computer company?" said Mr. White while he was looking at Edgar.

"I … I really don't know what to say?" replied Edgar.

"Look, Edgar, you have shown me all your faithfulness along this long time and I know you. You never made me sad or nervous even once and you always did your work very well. I need you to work by my side as I'm getting older day by day. But on the other hand, I crave your progress in life. I like you to be a successful person in the future. And I believe that you would be more successful if you grow up in a city environment rather than a village. You can experience new occasion that you may never face in a village. And I think working in a computer company is very good and it is a modern occupation. But all in all, everything depends on you. You can choose which way to take." said Mr. White as if a father speaking to his son.

Edgar was completely reticent. He faced a new chance after all events that had happened to him. All the events passed from his mind like a short film.

He had never been to a city before, and it made everything harder for him. He couldn't imagine how life is in a big city! Then, he asked his boss if he could go outside and think. Mr. White accepted and he left the shop and went toward the place that he had lost his sister; Lisa, there.

He sat on the bench and steeped in thinking. Nothing was around him except some trees and a narrow stream. Sound of the water was like background music. He was immersed in thinking about past, present, and future. He felt that Lisa is playing beyond the stream on the grass and he heard her voice. But it was just a daydream. There was no Lisa. There was no one except himself. There was just Edgar and his God.

So, he started speaking to his God. He called him loudly in his heart. Then his eyes burst into tears. If he went to city, he would leave Mr. White and his family who were like his own family; who had helped him every time in the hardest conditions when he did have no one. Who knows what would have happened to him if Mr. White hadn't helped him when he was swooned in front of his supermarket. What would have happened if Mr. White had seen him a vagrant like any other people? He owed his life to his boss. Not only once, he also owed his life to him when he injured himself fishing and his family saved him and took care of him for months. They looked after him like their own child.

Then, he remembered his friends; Bob, Teddy, and David. It was they who saved him from solitude. They helped him to find his sister every time. They were beside him in times of need. They were always loyal to him and also saved him in fishing incident. He would never forget that David put his life in danger to take him out of the river.

He remembered how Sara taught him painting with all her love. He even remembered the day that he bought that beautiful stone from that silly boy. That day everybody laughed at him, but he was happy buying a good present for his sister's birthday. Unfortunately, he never found his sister to give it to her, but he kept that stone with himself. It reminded him Lisa.

All these memories were laudable for him, even the bad ones. It was too hard for him to leave these memories and go to city. But on the other hand, he thought about future. He knew that he could reach his goals in the city better than in a village as Mr. White mentioned. Working in a computer company would let him know about technology and it was very good for him. Maybe he could continue his studying there. He could learn about business and learn how to be a rich and successful person.

At that time, Bob was passing there and when he saw Edgar, he went toward him.

"Hi, buddy. What are you doing here?" asked Bob.

"Hi, Bob. Nothing important. I was just thinking about something which has preoccupied me." replied Edgar.

"Can I ask what is that?" asked Bob.

"Sure!" Then, Edgar explained the story and continued, "Mr. White said that I can go there and work in that company if I wanted. And now, I don't know what to do."

"What kind of company is that?" asked Bob curiously.

"Computer; that is, computer business." answered Edgar.

"Fantastic! That is awesome. I love computers, unfortunately, I don't have any. And what is your opinion?" said Bob loudly.

"That is exactly my problem. I really don't know what to do?" replied Edgar.

"This is a great opportunity for you. I would go if I were in your shoes. You can work there, get known with computers, and maybe in the future you can be a computer engineer." said Bob and smiled.

"Come on, Bob! I'm not joking at all." said Edgar and stood up from the bench.

"I was serious. Where are you going so?" said Bob.

"I've been here a long time. I have to go back." answered Edgar.

"Okay. Let's go together." said Bob.

Then they left there and walked toward the shop. In the middle of path, Bob left Edgar and went home and Edgar again got alone. He was completely garbled and he was thinking and he didn't notice anything around him, even the big hole in front of him. Then his foot felt down inn it, but he didn't pay attention and he just went rest of the path lamely and slowly.

A mild wind was caressing his face softly. Dark clouds were upon his head in the sky and it seemed to rain. The birds were going to their nests on the top of trees to be safe from the rain. Rabbits were running under bushes and even pismires left their baits on the ground and they ran toward their formicary rapidly because terrible loud sounds of thunders worried everyone about a cloud-burst. When the first drops of rain kissed the land, scent of wet soil raised up. Then, these drops gave special beauty to flowers' petals and made them fresh and fragrant especially red roses. Getting wet, all the colors in the area got darker. Everything was beautiful and emotional.

There wasn't anyone outside except Edgar that was near the shop. He had completely drenched. His blond hair had become dark brown and his blue eyes shined more than ever before. His brown pants had got black and his boots were like bathing-tub.

When he entered the shop, Mr. White got shocked seeing him like that. He brought a towel and dried him rapidly, then took him beside the small electric heater. Edgar was sneezing hardly; it seemed he had got a slight cold. Mr. White made coffee and gave him a big cup of it and sat beside him. He was like a real father. He did everything as like as a real father does for his own son.

Edgar was still silent and didn't say any words. He had kept the hot cup in his hands. It made him warmer. Then Mr. White asked him about that subject to know his opinion.

"I couldn't decide what to do on my own, I ... I will obey what you say." said Edgar in a small voice and drank his coffee. Some small drops were still falling down from his hair.

"Okay. We will discuss it at home, tonight" said Mr. White and smiled slightly.

It wasn't a busy day for them in the shop and they left there earlier than usual time, and Mr. White asked Edgar to go home with him. This time Edgar accepted easily because they were going to speak about an important issue. Then they closed the shop and went toward home.

When Sara opened the door and saw Edgar beside his father, she got very happy and called her mother. Mary got happy seeing Edgar. Then she went to kitchen to make a special dinner for their special guest.

Sara went upstairs to her room and after a short while came back with a beautiful red dress. She had chosen her best dress to wear that night because Edgar was there. She was prettier and more graceful than ever before in that red dress and she looked taller. She had put her hair on her shoulders. Her cheeks had become red and pink. Her lips below her small nose had a very beautiful shape. Her necklace was shining above her small breasts, on her neck. When she was coming down the stairs, she took all Edgar's attention with her beauty. Edgar was staring at her as he hadn't seen such a pretty girl before. She also had a picture in her hand.

She came down, sat beside Edgar and showed him her last painting and then explained about that to him. It was a picture of lonely boy that was staring at sky. That boy was Edgar and he was speaking with his God in that picture. Edgar got surprised by seeing that picture and congratulated on her proficiency. It was the best picture that he had ever seen in his life.

When Mary came out of the kitchen and saw Edgar and Sara speaking lovingly, got very happy. And also she got surprised seeing that Sara had worn her best dress that night. She had made different kinds of foods. There were Spaghetti, colcannon, chicken and rice and some other delicious foods. The table was decorated very beautiful. They sat around it and started eating those delicious foods.

Mr. White started to thank his wife for her delicious food as usual. He was eating voraciously whatever was before him. Sara was swallowing long ropes of spaghetti with her narrow lips. And Edgar was busy eating colcannon; he loved it very much.

When they finished dinner, Mr. White gathered them to speak about an important subject. Then, he explained about the situation that Edgar had. When Sara heard the first sentence about Edgar's leaving, she got worried, but she kept silent to listen to the rest of her father's words. And so did her mother when she heard it. It was hard for them to hear about his going because they had got used to him hard. With Edgar's presence, Mary had a son and Sara had a very kind brother. He had become a member of their family. How could they think about his absence? The saddest person was Sara because she loved him more than a brother.

Mr. White explained everything completely and asked Edgar to tell his opinion. Edgar was silent and he didn't know what to say. The clock on the wall showed ten o'clock at night. What a hard and depressing night it was for them! They all stared at each other without saying a word and nobody had anything to say except keeping silent. After a while, Edgar broke the silence and tried to express his opinion.

"At first, let me thank you all because of all your kindnesses toward me along this long time that I know you. I don't know where I was now if you weren't in my adventure. You saved me, you looked after me when I was sick, you gave me work, food and a place to live and sleep, and you requited my family's absence and you didn't let me feel lonely even for a short while. You gave me all kindnesses that parents could give to their child. You looked at me as your own child and never discriminated between me and Sara. You taught me how to work and be a real man to control my life.

But beyond all these, I had a very bad history. Now I am an orphan. I lost my mother, Venus. I wouldn't want anything else from the whole world if she were with me now. If those horrible events hadn't happened to me, now I could have continued my school like all other boys and girl in my age. I could continue my studying and be an engineer, a doctor, or a teacher. But after that calamity, my life changed and now I have to live in a different way. But facing this situation, I think that God hasn't forgotten me yet and I think he wants to examine me again. I crave to requite all my bad lucks in the past trying to be a successful person in the future." said Edgar.

"Edgar, my dear, I'm sure you can be whatever you want because I know your abilities and your effort when you work. You always did your work better than I expected and you never made a mistake. Furthermore, I grasp your feelings about your past and what had happened to you. I appreciate your tendency to be an important man in the future for yourself and your society. And I have to tell that you would be more successful in a city than here, in a village. You could improve there more than here, in all aspects. And I can't stop you here to work in the shop; to achieve my goals and to be comfortable. Your success is more important to me." Mr. said White.

Sara was in the corner of the room and was very sad that night. She couldn't believe that Edgar was about to leave them to live in another place, in the city. She wanted to cry and ask him not to go, but she couldn't do that. She was deeply got used to Edgar more than she could imagine and she loved him as her best and dearest friend. She had passed all his best times with him and beside him. The time Edgar was sick, was her best time, not because he was in bed, but because she could sit beside him and talk with him for hours. How beautiful painting was beside him! She liked to go with him to city, but it was impossible, and she had just to believe his leaving. She liked to speak with him that night, but she didn't know what to say.

"Where is he going to work there?" asked Mary.

"That's my friend's company, Mr. Thomas. He is a real gentleman and also eminent in the city. I'm sure he would love Edgar, too. Edgar will be a big computer engineer. We'll go tomorrow morning." answered Mr. White.

"I always wish his success, too. Although I got used to him a lot, and like him to stay with us, but his success is more important." smiled Mary.

Then she went to Sara, sat beside her and asked, "Why are you sitting here? Come and join us."

"Nothing special, Mom… I'm just thinking." replied Sara.

"What are you thinking about?" asked Mary again.

"That's not important." answered Sara in a small voice.

"Okay. I don't know what is passing in your mind, but come and sit beside us. You heard; they are going tomorrow morning. Let's be with each other tonight." said Mary and took Lisa's hand and they went to Mr. White and Edgar.

Edgar and Sara stared at each other in a big silence. There wasn't any word in the world to outbreak their emotions that time. Sara's parents were confused about her actions that night. She was very silent unlike her usual behavior that she spoke a lot. But that night, she just looked at them without saying a word.

Only the second-handle of the old clock on the wall made sounds in the room, and nothing else. Suddenly, they heard a cat's sound mewing behind the door. It was Sara's mignon brown cat. She went to the kitchen and found some food to give to her. Then she went out. Mary asked Edgar to join Sara.

She was playing with her cuddly brown cat in the middle of the garden beside the small pond. Edgar went closer and stood beside Sara. But she didn't look at him and continued feeding her cat not paying attention to him. They were alone in the garden under the white light of the moon. It was cold and all the plants had lost their flowers in the garden. The ground was covered with dried leaves and the grass had changed to yellow.

"I don't understand why you are treating like this, tonight. You should perceive me; I have to go. Otherwise, I liked to stay beside you and my dear friends, here. Surely, I will miss you." Edgar said in a small voice

"I know. You want to reach your goals. You want to be an important person. But you are selfish and you just watch yourself without considering others." said Sara and continued feeding her cat.

"It is hard for me to leave you, your parents, my friends and this memorable village, believe me. I would never forget your kindnesses. I would think about you wherever I go. I will come back. I promise. I can never forget you, Sara." replied Edgar while looking at Sara's beautiful eyes with the reflection of moonlight in them. She was more beautiful under moon light. She had become like an angel. A mild and cool wind was combing her straight blonde hair softly. That scene couldn't be explained by any word.

"I'll miss you, Edgar. You have played the role of a brother or the best friend for me and you didn't let me feel alone. Now, it's hard for me to become alone again. Promise to come back soon." said Sara while she was about to burst into tears; she was very soft-hearted. Edgar kissed her cheek and took her inside. Sara got very happy about his kissing. It was for the first time that Edgar kissed her. It was the sweetest kiss she had ever experienced in her life.

Next morning, the old tree's bare branches were scratching the glass of windows and it made a slight sound in the room. The light of the sun had reached the front walls of the room and everywhere was bright and shiny. The special smell of the morning had been blown among all the rooms and the sparrows were singing morning song on the trees.

Mr. White's car switched on. It woke Sara up. She jumped out of her bed immediately and went near the window. She looked outside and saw that her mother is shaking hand to her father and Edgar that were in the lorry leaving the home. She ran downstairs rapidly without changing her nightclothes. When she reached her mother, Mary was coming inside with a piece of handkerchief on her hands. Mary dried her tears.

"Where did they go?" asked Sara hurriedly.

"Your father drove Edgar to city. They went where we spoke about last night." answered Mary.

"Why didn't you wake me up?" asked Sara her mother angrily.

"Your father and I thought that it's better and easier for." answered Mary in small voice.

Sara got too sad and hugged her mother firmly. Her tiny and beautiful eyes burst into tears on Mary's warm bosom.

They both were sorry of Edgar's going and they had to continue their life like before his coming to their family. Sara turned her face up and looked at her mother not winking. Then she left Mary and went near the window and looked outside to the road. The road was vacant and there weren't any one or any cars. She just saw her brown cat that was getting closer to her. She ran outside and caught the cat and took it inside with herself. Maybe, she had to pass her solitude times by playing with that mignon cat. She didn't go to school that day and stayed at home all the day beside her mother.

Chapter 4

Mr. White was driving toward city and Edgar was sitting beside him, in silence. He was just staring at right outside-mirror to look back. He was sad while village's picture was getting smaller and smaller in the mirror, and after a while, he couldn't see any picture of the village in the mirror, any more. The road sides were surrounded by tall trees and they were driving under their shadows. Sheep and cows were grazing on the roadsides and a young shepherd was taking care of them. Edgar shook hand for shepherd and he replied tempestuously. Mr. White was driving slowly and with composure while he was signing a classic song. He always enjoyed his singing and liked to sing.

"Do you like driving?" asked Mr. White.

"I don't know, I have never thought about it." replied Edgar.

"You will learn. If you were in the village, maybe you would never need to learn it because in the village, most of people use horses and carts, but in the city everybody uses a car. Without cars, they are feeble." said Mr. White and laughed.

Passing time, as they got nearer to city, the environment changed. Small wooden houses changed to modern buildings. Instead of sheep and any other animals, they were big and huge companies and factories.

They were all surprising to Edgar since he had never been to a city before, and he hadn't ever seen before what he saw that day. Everywhere was full of different kinds of people with different styles. Roads and streets were full of cars and Mr. White was complaining about them as usual. He always thought of city residents as poor people. He never liked to change his calm life in the village with a noisy life in city.

He directly drove toward his friend's company. It was a big company about the city center.

"Okay. It's here. You can get out of car" said Mr. White looking at the building in front of him. On the top of the building had been written in capital letters: Thomas Computer Center. It had been named Thomas because the name of the company's owner was Mr. Thomas who was Mr. White's close friend. Edgar got off the car while he had his small luggage in his right hand.

They entered the building together and went to Mr. Thomas's office in the last floor. When Mr. Thomas saw his old friend he got very happy and welcomed them. He asked his worker to bring them two special cups of coffee. Two old friends started speaking to each other warmly. Edgar was partly attentive to the office and partly to his thereafter boss, Mr. Thomas. It seemed that he was a good and kind person. He laughed loudly but very soon he stopped it and returned to his serious gesture. He was heavy and he had a shaped moustache upon his thick lips. He had round black eyes with thick eyebrows and he looked very serious. He had some small narrow wrinkles on his big forehead and he was a bit bald.

His office was very big and all the walls were decorated with the pictures of the famous painters of the world. When they finished their long greeting, Mr. White looked at Edgar and spoke about him to Mr. Thomas.

"This is the boy whom I talked about last time. Edgar is very polite, obedient, and active; he would always be better than you expect from him. He helped me in my supermarket and I hadn't had any shop-boy like him before. It's hard for me to lose him in my shop, but I want his success because I love him as my own son. I think he would be more successful if he lives and works here rather than in the village. And best of all, he would work in a computer company and he would learn about technology and modern life." said Mr. White and smiled.

"He seems like everything you said. And also I'm assured about him because you have brought him here, my dear friend. I would do everything for him that I could and he can learn about computers, here. I give you my word on it; he would improve here better than anywhere else." said Mr. Thomas kindly. Hearing his words, Edgar got delighted and hopeful.

"I know, my friend. I rely on you because I know you since my childhood and I remember that you always did what you wanted." said Mr. White.

"I have really missed village and those times." replied Mr. Thomas and sighed.

"Okay. I have to go back to village soon to do my works. My shop is close since morning until now. God knows how many costumers I have lost. I leave you alone. I hope success for both of you…" Mr. White said and stood up slowly from his chair.

"I got happy to see you again, my old friend. I will take care of Edgar. Promise to come and visit us whenever you come here for shopping." said Mr. Thomas.

"Be sure, I will. Good bye." said Mr. White and walked toward corridor. Edgar stood up, ran after him and took his hand. When Mr. White turned back, Edgar hugged him firmly and burst into tears. Mr. White sat down on his knees and dragged his hand on Edgar's hair and slowly told him: "Don't cry, boy. You are a man, now. I promise, I will come and visit you whenever I come here for shopping. And you promise to be a good boy. Okay?"

"I will miss you and your family. Convey my regards to Mary, Sara, and My friends. I promise I will do my best here to requite all your kindnesses." said Edgar in a small voice. Then they stood up, Mr. White went and disappeared between workers who were in the corridor.

The company was very crowded and full of workers from all ages and sexes. Women wore short maroon skirts till upon their knees and white formal blouses with the brand of company on their chests and men wore maroon suits and formal white shirts. Most of them were looking at Edgar strangely since he was a very young person standing there.

Edgar came back to Mr. Thomas's office and sat on a chair. Mr. Thomas was busy speaking on the telephone at his grand brown desk. He was speaking about money, not in small numbers, but in hundreds, thousands, and even millions. These were strange to Edgar because he always heard about money in tens or outside in hundreds.

Mr. Thomas was still deep in numbers even after his phone call. Then suddenly, he noticed that Edgar was in front of him on the chair. He forgot all his works, came, and sat beside Edgar.

"Excuse me. Everybody calls me and all they ask is money, money, and money. No one ask about my temper. No one invites me for dinner in a restaurant to eat salmon with French fries. Nobody buys me a ticket and invites me to a theater to watch one of the Shakespeare's wonderful plays on the dark stage between people. I love cinema. Do you?" said Mr. Thomas.

"I ... I don't know, sir. I haven't been to a cinema before." replied Edgar in a very small voice.

"I will take you. You know, I have two sons. Both are married and live in other cities far away from here. They don't visit their old parents more often. So, my wife and I are alone at home. My wife doesn't like cinema or going to a restaurant for dinner, so, I have no one to go out with. You will be my friend, Edgar..." said Mr. Thomas and walked toward the window to look out.

It seemed he got sad when he spoke about his sons. He was very rich, but too alone. His wife didn't like going out with him or eating dinner in a restaurant. Her only hobby was playing cards with the women in their neighborhood. His wife was about fifty, but behaved like an 80-year-old woman and always complained about everything. But Mr. Thomas loved her anyway because he had passed all his lovely days in youth with her and beside her. Loves get old; loves get weak, but never die. They still loved each other, but their love's fever had become weak and slight. Their love's huge fire had changed to a small candle's blaze that could be put out with a mild blow, but it was burning; although weak.

But Mr. Thomas's behavior was different from his wife's. He didn't like solitude. He liked going to movies, theaters, or a restaurant to have dinner, but he didn't have any one to join him. On the other hand, he was too busy with his company. He worked hard not in need of money as he had already a lot. But he didn't work for money anymore and he just did it as a hobby.

"Let me show you the whole building and the different parts of the company. Okay?" said Mr. Thomas.

"Sure, sir" replied Edgar.

They went out of the office and walked in the corridor. All the employees stood straight and said hello when they saw their manager; then they continued their job soon after Mr. Thomas replied with a simple nod.

Mr. Thomas showed all the floors of the building and all parts of the company to Edgar. At last, they reached the second floor; a dormitory for foreign engineers and employees to rest. They walked to the end of the corridor and stopped at the last door.

"It's your room. It is small, but comfortable." said Mr. Thomas.

"Thank you, sir. Not small! Even it is very big for me." replied Edgar.

"Okay. You can take rest today. I will tell you what to do tomorrow." said Mr. Thomas and left.

Edgar entered the room, put his small bag in a corner and lay down on the bed. The bed was very comfortable and soft and he couldn't compare it with his hard bed behind the refrigerator in Mr. White's shop. He walked toward the small window, drew the brown curtain back and looked outside. The other side of the street, he saw a big guidance school and a park beside it. The street was replete with different kinds of cars and vehicles and a large number of people were walking on the pavements. Most of the women were coming back from shopping; they had large plastic bags in their hands.

Edgar opened the window to smell fresh air, but he didn't smell anything but smoke, so he closed it and went back to his bed. Then, he opened his bag and took out his belongings. While he was taking out his things, he found his shiny stone and started at it. It was really beautiful and shiny and it didn't seem to be worthless. Any way, he cleaned it and put in a corner on the desk and collected his other things. He found a novel and started reading it. It was Sara's gift.

After some hours, it was getting darker and the sun was greeting the moon and the stars. The lights in the street turned on and a beautiful scene was made at night. Edgar was tired and he went to bed to sleep soon. He wanted to wake up early in the morning before Mr. Thomas come to his room. He lay down on his soft bed and closed his eyes slowly.

He was fast asleep, and after a short while, he started dreaming as usual. His mind was occupied with memories which changed to night dreams when he slept. He always dreamed about that horrible night that he lost his parents. He saw Lisa in his mother's bosom and playing with her. Then suddenly, he woke up with terrible sound of a horn in the street. Hi face was cold sweat. He dried his face with his sleeve and then tried to sleep again. But this time, he couldn't sleep and he thought about poor Lisa. He moved in the bed for a while and after some minutes slept.

Everywhere was silent and nobody was in the building except people in the second floor and the watchman in the first floor behind the entrance door. It was hardly raining that night and all the streets were wet. Clouds had covered the moon and the stars, and none of them were seen. Rain drops kissed the window's glass and then rolled down on the wall.

Next morning, Edgar got up early like when he was in the village. He had learnt to wake up early and he couldn't stay in bed until late. It was about a quarter to seven in the morning and he thought that he had got up earlier than others, but when he went near the window and looked at the street, he saw that hundreds of people were there. Some of them were walking and some others were driving on the street. Shopkeepers were opening their shops. Students were going to school. Gardeners were watering the park. Everywhere was crowded, replete with people, and cars. When he saw all these, he got that he hadn't got up that much early.

He turned back to his bed and changed his clothes. Then he waited for Mr. Thomas to come. Until his boss came, he cleaned his room. Then, he went in front of the mirror and combed his hair and fixed his clothes.

It was about eight o'clock when someone knocked on the door. Edgar stood up and went to the door. Opening the door, he saw Mr. Thomas standing in front of him.

"Good morning, sir." said Edgar.

"Good morning. Did you enjoy your room? Did you sleep well?" asked Mr. Thomas.

"Yes. Everything was good. I hadn't slept on such comfortable bed before." answered Edgar.

"Okay. I see that you are ready?" said Mr. Thomas and smiled.

"Yes. I tried to wake up soon and get ready before you came." answered Edgar.

"Well! I appreciate it. It seems that you are an active boy as Mr. White said. I hope you always continue this manner." said Mr. Thomas.

"I will always do my best, sir." replied Edgar.

"Now let's go with me. First, we will have a small breakfast, and then I will show you where you should work." said Mr. Thomas and turned back and walked to the corridor.

Edgar went out of his room and closed the door and walked behind Mr. Thomas. After eating a small meal, they went upstairs. They exited the elevator in the last floor. Edgar was garbled because the last floor was Mr. Thomas's own office and he couldn't realize that what he would do there beside his boss.

Mr. Thomas turned right to a room before he reach his own office. It was next to his room. Two men were working there. One of them was tall and thin with short hair and the other was fat and short. When Mr. Thomas entered the room, they stood up immediately and greeted him warmly. Then, they looked at Edgar.

"Here is the place that you will work, Edgar." said Mr. Thomas while his right hand was on Edgar's left shoulder. He continued, "You will help John and Robby here. They are my best engineers in the company. You should always obey them."

“Yes, sir.” replied Edgar in a small voice.

“You, John! He will help you as an apprentice for a while. Then, I will move him to another place. Edgar is very active and polite and so dear for me. Try to treat him well.” said Mr. Thomas

“Yes, sir. I assure you.” replied John and looked at Edgar and smiled.

“Okay, Edgar. I am going to my office. You can start your work, right now. I’m in my office. You can visit me whenever you want. If you face any problem, come and tell me. I will come at noon and take you to Stephen. He will teach you computer. Now, go and start your work with John and Robby.” said Mr. Thomas and left the room.

Edgar was still standing in front of the door looking at his toes. He was a bit embarrassed. John and Robby were looking at him. They thought that what such a young boy can do. But they had to obey their boss and give Edgar something to do. John stood up from his chair and walked toward Edgar.

“What was your name?” asked John.

“Edgar, sir” replied Edgar.

“You needn’t call me Sir. You can call me John. How old are you, Edgar?” said John.

“I’m about eleven, sir.” replied Edgar.

“I said you needn’t call me sir. You can call us John and Robby. Okay?” said John.

“Yes, John” replied Edgar having a small smile on his face.

“I have to tell you that I don’t know what you can do here. But actually now you can help Robby and me take things to other rooms. Is it good?” said John.

“Of course.” replied Edgar.

Then Edgar went and sat beside John’s desk on a chair and did his and Robby’s stuffs whenever they wanted. He looked exactly at what they were doing behind their computers, but he couldn’t understand anything as he hadn’t worked with any computers before.

When John got free, he started asking questions from Edgar about him and his private life. When he heard about Edgar's past, he got sorry for him and he looked at him strangely.

It was about twelve o'clock. Mr. Thomas came and took Edgar to Stephen in the fifth floor. Stephen was a computer engineer and he taught new employers about computer. When they entered his room, he was busy with his computer as usual. Even he didn't notice their coming. Mr. Thomas knocked on the door. He looked at the door and saw his boss beside a young boy. He stood up immediately and greeted them.

"Hi, Stephen. I see you were busy with your computer as usual." said Mr. Thomas.

"Yes, sir. I was searching for a file in the Internet." replied Stephen.

They started speaking about the file that Stephen was searching in the Internet. Edgar was silent as most of the words that they were using were unknown for him; Internet, file, download and other technical words. All these words were unknown for him. They spoke for a while with each other. Then, Mr. Thomas turned his face toward Edgar and showed him to Stephen.

"This is Edgar. I want you to teach him computer. I want you to try your best. He has to learn soon about computer." said Mr. Thomas seriously.

"I'll do that, sir." replied Stephen.

Stephen and Edgar made a short but warm greeting. Then Mr. Thomas and Edgar left the room. It was time to have lunch. They went out of the building.

"I want to take you to an Italian restaurant at the end of this street. Its foods are traditional and very delicious. They have a kind of special food that is wonderful. I love it. I'm sure you will enjoy it, too. And also, all the workers are Italian there. They are very kind and gentlemen. You love go there?" said Mr. Thomas.

"Sure, sir." replied Edgar while he was happy that he is going to have lunch with his new boss in a special restaurant.

They walked on the pavement together. When Mr. Thomas was walking with Edgar, he remembered his sons when they were Edgar's age.

"About Twenty years ago, I walked this street with my sons by my side. I held their hands and I took them to park. They loved playing slide. I always had to buy chocolate ice cream for them. How beautiful days were those times! That time I didn't have this company. I didn't have much money, but I had a happy life with my family. I used to work in an electric instruments repair shop.

My boss was an old man. He is dead now. God bless him. He was the teacher of my life. He always advised me to have a goal and try to reach my goal at any price. He taught me that the life is worthless without having a goal. He said that each person should have a goal in life, and follow it up to the end." said Mr. Thomas.

"What was your goal, sir?" asked Edgar.

"My goal was what you are seeing now; this computer company. I loved computer and digital world and at first I didn't know anything about it. But then, I learnt it and achieved it step by step. Keep in mind that you have to go step by step. You can never achieve your goal over a night. You have to try days and nights. You shouldn't get disappointed with a loss. When you are lost in a step, you should forget it and stand up again and continue your way to reach the goal.

I remember that some nights I slept just two or three hours. I read all books and new magazines about computer along the nights. I never forget those days and nights. I was full of energy. I craved to be rich. I believed that rich people can achieve whatever they want. I thought that money solves all the problems and makes all the wishes and dreams come true. I craved to make a good life for myself and my family like everybody that loves to have a good and comfortable life without any problems. I tried to be rich to make my sons successful.

I passed all my time working and working. I worked days and nights to be a rich man. But unfortunately, I forgot my sons an even my wife. I worked for them, but not in a right way. Sixteen years ago, I established this company in a small office with only a secretary. My business was very small, but I was too busy with that because I wanted to extend it as much as possible. Too many nights I worked in the office until late and even I slept there. Day by day, my business got stronger and bigger and I was getting nearer to my goal. But on the other hand, I was losing something valuable against getting closer to my business goal. I had forgotten my family. I had forgotten my sons. I had forgotten my wife." said Mr. Thomas in a sad voice.

"Why do you say that? Why do you think that you lost your family?" asked Edgar curiously.

"I lost them because I wasn't beside them as I used to. I wasn't that kind father like before to my sons. I didn't have any time to take them anywhere. I thought that they just needed money for their future life, whereas they needed a kind father to give them kindness and attention.

In a period of time, we concentrate on our goal with all our attention and unfortunately we forget other aspects of our life. Trying to reach one thing, we lose other essentials. In that that time, not only having a goal is not good but also it destroys your life. That time, you regret all the things you have lost.

Passing time, my company was expanded more and more and I got too busy with my work. When it became a big company after six years, then it started expanding in a way that I couldn't control it even if I wanted. Every day new orders, every day new employees and other news.

I really wanted my sons to work in this company beside me. But after they got married they went far away and didn't stay with me. One of them is working in his own farm beside his wife and the other is a history teacher. They don't earn too much money, but they love their jobs and they work with all their hearts. They dedicate a big part of their time to their children; what I couldn't realize and do for them.

When they left me, I realized that I was wrong in my life. I tried to be rich to make them successful in their future lives, but I chose the wrong way. I don't say that money is bad. But emotions are more essential in the life. I had to dedicate more time to them to make them nearer to me. Now, they are far from me either in distance or in our family relationship. They come here and visit me and their mother each season.

But I love to see them every day." said Mr. Thomas sadly and took off his hat and played with it in his hands.

He got calmer when he could speak about his heartaches to a person after years. Along these long years, he didn't know anyone reliable to speak about his heartaches to. He was overjoyed that there was someone honest and innocent like Edgar whom he could speak with easily.

When they were crossing a narrow street, a speedy car was about to take them over. The rough driver put his hand on the horn and blew it so long. They stopped at their place and the driver passed them with a rude face.

"You see? Everyone is about to fight! We can't even cross a street calmly." Said Mr. Thomas and wore a small smile on his wrinkled and colorless lips.

They walked for a while and reached the restaurant. Mr. Thomas looked at himself at the outer window of the restaurant and fixed his coat and tie. Then, they entered the restaurant. It was a restaurant completely different from other modern ones in the city. It was decorated traditionally and everything was old around it. There were antique and golden icons. Wooden seats were designed adroitly and the floor was covered by beautiful and original Iranian carpets and a classical music had made the ambience more emotional.

When Mr. Thomas entered, the owner of the restaurant came toward him and greeted him warmly. He guided them to their seat. Mr. Thomas was known there since he often went there. Everything was new and lovely for Edgar. He hadn't seen such a place before and he was very happy of being there. The waiter came and asked for their order. Mr. Thomas without looking at the menu ordered his favorite food for two and then he turned to Edgar and said, "Do you enjoy here?"

"Surely I do, sir. Everything is lovely here" replied Edgar.

"Yes. Here is really lovely. I always get calm when I'm here. Here is completely different from the other new and modern restaurants. I believe that in new restaurants they just do their best to make new foods to face people with new comes. But here foods are original and delicious. And also, people who come here usually are artists from different majors of art; often musicians, novelists and poets. They always discuss art, love or other sweet aspects of life. They never speak about money. Sometimes, they discuss a novel or a poem for hours and give their opinions to each other. Often a poet comes and reads his newest poem to his friends with all his love and emotion and others encourage him. I think that moment he receives all he wants. But in my life, always numbers and dollars filled my mind and I didn't enjoy any other beauties of my life.

I regret all the time that I have lost running after money without paying any attention to anything else. I have to say that I couldn't utilize my money. I don't know what would happen to this large quantity of my private property after my death. I am sure my sons wouldn't accept this property because they don't need it. They enjoy their lives with their low earnings. Sometimes, I think that my goal was wrong. Then I think that the way that I had chosen to reach my goal was wrong. And sometimes, I think even having a goal and paying much attention to it is wrong. " Said Mr. Thomas and sighed.

Edgar listened to him carefully. He thought that he could use Mr. Thomas's experiences in his life. He could follow good experiences and refuse the bad ones. He could feel that even in the second day of being in the city, he had learnt more about life.

Chapter 5

Sara came back from school and entered home with a very sad face. She wasn't the happy and cute girl that she used to. Mary was in the back yard busy feeding the docks and hens. When she came back inside, she saw Sara's school bag on the sofa, but she wasn't there herself. She looked at the kitchen and living room, but she couldn't find her. She went upstairs to Sara's room. Sara was looking out of the window while she was playing with her bear doll in her hands. She had fully focused on outside even she didn't notice her mother's coming in. She had stared at the yellow falling leaves. She fallowed one with her eyes till it laid on the ground and then she followed another falling leaf. Mary looked at her in deep silence. She was standing at the door cradling looking directly at her daughter. Sara got tired of following leaves and turned back to lie on her bed. The moment of her turn, she saw her mother standing at the door looking at her.

"Hi, Mom. Why are you standing there?" said Sara.

"I was looking at my sweetie daughter. And you? You were so busy that you didn't notice my coming!" said Mary and smiled.

"I was looking at the falling leaves. I am really tired. I feel lonely. Nothing is enjoyable for me anymore." answered Sara sadly in a small voice.

"I know what you mean. And I know you have missed Edgar. He was a friend, companion, and a brother for you. You got use to him firmly and so did I. But we have to accept his absence. He will come, soon." said Mary this and went beside her daughter. She sat beside her on the bed. She took Sara's hands and held them firmly; then hugged her warmly with all her love. Sara put her head on her mother's bosom. Mary started combing her hairs with her fingers.

"I have really missed Edgar. He was the best and the kindest friend that I have ever had in my life. He was honest and innocent." said Sara.

"He faced a lot of misfortunes in his life, especially in the parts of his life when he would start getting into society. But everything changed for him. Now, he has to live in another way; and maybe he doesn't like it. Every child likes to live beside his family. Every child loves to hug his mother. Every child loves to rely on his father. But he lacks all of these. I hope after all these misfortunes, he achieves everything he loves and wants." said Mary.

"When would he come back?" asked Sara fervently.

"I don't know my dear daughter. But your father promised to take him here to visit us soon." smiled Mary.

"Can I ask something that refers to you and dad?" asked Sara curiously.

"Of course, my sweetie." replied Mary.

"How did you and dad meet each other for the first time?" asked Sara.

"Ah... you asked about the sweetest part of my life. I would never forget that time. Your father was a young tall man with black hair and he was very handsome. Most of the young girls in the village knew him because of his handsomeness. He worked in the supermarket of his old uncle. The shop in which he is working today is come down by inheritance to him, from his uncle. After his uncle's death, he became the owner of the shop. I met him for the first time in the supermarket. I was about nineteen and he was about twenty six. When I entered his shop, we both looked at each other strangely. He collected everything I needed immediately and asked me if I let him take them home. But I didn't accept and I did it myself. After that day, whenever I went to his shop he left all other costumers and first of all collected my things. Passing time, I felt that I had taken his attention. If truth be told, he had taken my attention, too. After that, I always tried to go to his shop even when I didn't have any necessary shopping. I went there and just buy some small thing, but we spoke for a long time. Little by little, our relationship got closer and warmer. After that, sometimes we met each other outside." said Mary and steeped in her memories.

"Who first expressed his or her love?" asked Sara curiously.

"Of course, your father did. One day, your father asked me for a walk in the jungle around the village. When we were walking slowly through the trees on the soft green grass, suddenly, he jumped in front of me and took my hands softly. I was completely shocked. He asked me to close my eyes. I accepted and closed my eyes firmly. It was about to rain and I felt some drops of rain on my face. It wasn't too much rain, but the fresh scent of wet soil was great that time. I think your father had chosen the best time to explain his love to me. My emotions in that beautiful weather had been thousand times stranger than ever before. My eyes still were closed that suddenly, I felt a big bouquet in my hands. When I opened my eyes I saw different kinds of beautiful flowers in my hand. I hadn't seen such beautiful bouquet in my life." Mary was explaining when suddenly, Sara ran in on her speech and again asked a question with all her curiosity, "Did you notice what father meant when he gave you the bouquet?"

"Yes. That time, I could feel his love strongly. He wanted to say about his love, but it was clear that he was shy. We looked at each other's eyes for a while. Your father was going to start speaking when a big and loud thunder struck and made us frightened. And then it started to rain hard. Increasing the rain, we left each other and went home. When I reached home, I dried myself and then went to my room and thought about your father whole the night. I couldn't sleep that night. I regretted the beautiful bouquet that I left on the ground as I was frightened of the thunder." said Mary.

"So, what happened then?" asked Sara.

Mary continued, "Next early morning, I went to shop. Your father was coughing badly. I asked him; why are you coughing such badly? He answered; I walked for a long time under the rain after you left me and went home. When I heard this I got so sorry for him. About a week passed from that day. One Sunday, I went shopping to his shop; when he finished collecting my things, he put a note in the bag and smiled to me. His smile was very sweet for me, that day. When I went outside, I put my hand in the bag and took out the paper immediately."

"What did the note say?" asked Sara.

"It said a big I LOVE YOU in red. I have still kept that piece of paper. That was the first time he expressed his love. When he proposed me from my family, your grandparents were completely agreed with that. After that time, we are living beside each other for these long years and never did our love fade; even it became more and more, day after day." answered Mary still deep in memories.

"Should always first men express their love to women?" asked Sara.

"Not always! But often men are prior. It is the nature of love and almost no one could change it. In some cases, girls express their love when they love someone very much. More than their pride and prejudice. But often it makes troubles for girls." replied Mary.

"What kind of troubles?" asked Sara.

"When a girl expresses her love to a boy, there are some boys who misuse them. Or they think they can treat the girl who loves them however they desire." Answered Marry and looked at the clock and said, "Ah! Now, it's time your father came. Let me go and make lunch ready. You, go and change your clothes and come downstairs for lunch."

Sara opened her closet and chose a blouse and changed her clothes. She stood up in front of the mirror and looked at herself for a while. She combed her long blonde hair and then tied it behind her head. She was growing up and either more beautiful day by day. Her neck was getting taller and her breasts were getting bigger than before. She was getting an adult girl. When she heard her father's car, she went beside the window and looked outside. It was Mr. White coming back from work. She ran to downstairs and waited in the living room to kiss her father when he came in.

Next morning, when Sara was going to school, she saw a man with a motorcycle standing beyond the fence of their house. As she got closer, she saw that it was Mr. Richards the mail-carrier of the village. She ran toward him and opened the gate, immediately. They knew each other very well. Mr. Richards always transfer Sara's paintings to different painting festivals.

She jumped in front of him and said in a sweet voice: "Good morning, Uncle Richards" Mr. Richards raised his head and saw a pretty girl with school uniform standing in front of him.

"How are you, sweetie?" said Mr. Richards kindly.

"I'm fine." replied Sara.

"What were you doing in this early morning in the yard?" mail-carrier asked.

"Look! I have put on my school dress, so I'm going to school, uncle." replied Sara tricking and laughed.

"Wow! You are right, sweetie. I'm getting older and older day by day and I don't notice anything around me. If I were younger, I would show you naughty girl. Now, close your eyes. Wait and let me find your letter to give you. I have a lot of letters to deliver, today." said Mr. Richards and looked in his bag for Sara's letter.

"Last time I sent one of my paintings to a festival. Have I won a prize?" asked Sara curiously.

"No! This time you have a letter from a person. I forgot his name. Let me find the letter; I will tell you." replied mail-carrier while he was looking for letter in his green bag. Sara thought about the sender. "Who would send me a letter?" she asked herself. She was staring at mail-carrier's hands that were searching in the bag for letter. Then, Mr. Richards took out two letters and read one of them hardly. It seemed he was already old enough to retire.

"From Edgar to Dear Sara." he read.

"Edgar? Are you sure? Oh my god! Edgar has sent me a letter. Thank you Mr. Richards, thank you." said Sara happily and took the letter from mail-carrier. She wanted to leave him soon to read the letter on her way to school. But when she wanted to leave, Mr. Richards stopped her and showed another letter and said, "This is another letter from Edgar to his friends. Can you give it to his friends? Do you meet them?"

"Yeah, of course. I'll take it to them." she said this and left him.

"How happy she got! I'd better go and deliver other letters." the mail-carrier thought. Then he sat on his old motorcycle and rode away from there. He couldn't even control the motorcycle carefully and he went from one side of the road to the other side while he was singing.

On the other end of the road, Sara opened her letter. She couldn't even stop to arrive at school and read her letter there. He opened the letter and kept it in her hands. The wind was blowing and didn't let her keep the letter straight, but she tried to read it at any rate. There letter read;

Dear Sara,

I am writing to tell you about my life in this short time in the city. I liked to write you sooner, but I didn't have any opportunity to do that till now. Everything is very good and comfortable, here. I'm working in a very big company, in a very beautiful and modern building, and everything here is completely different from the village. My new manager here, Mr. Thomas, is a very kind and good person. He gave me a job next to his own office. I'm working beside John and Robby. They are very good to me, too.

In the afternoons, Stephen teaches me computer. He is the teacher for new employees in the company. He knows everything about computer. I will tell you more about computer, in my next letters. As I said before, my new manager is very gentleman. But unfortunately, he is very alone and a bit old. His wife doesn't have any word with him and his sons are in other cities far from here.

He took me to cinema and a very beautiful restaurant. I would speak about all of these when I meet you. I have really missed you and Mr. and Mrs. White; and also my friends. I have written another letter for them. I will try to come there and meet all of you as soon as possible. Please, give my best regards to your mother and Mr. White. I will be waiting for your letter. With love. Edgar.

She loved to read more, but it was the end of the letter by the signature of Edgar Oliver. She closed the letter and put it in her pocket. When she raised up her head and looked around, she noticed she had passed her school not knowing it, since she had steeped in the letter. She was overjoyed that day. When her school finished, she went to Teddy to give the second letter to him. His father's carpentry was on the path.

She went in front of the carpentry and stood up outside beside a tree. Teddy was busy working hard with woods. His father was beside him. Sara raised her hand to call him, but Teddy was busy and didn't notice her. Then, she went in and called him out.

"Hi, Sara. What are you doing here?" said Teddy.

"Hi. I have good news for you." said Sara happily.

"What is your good news?" asked Teddy curiously.

"I have a letter for you, Bob, and David. It's from Edgar." said Sara.

"Wow! I've really missed him. I got very happy with this and I'm sure Bob and David will be happy, too." said Teddy happily.

"I have to go, see you later." said Sara and left there.

Teddy went back to the shop and asked his father whether he could leave or not. When his father agreed, he immediately changed his work clothes and wore his coat and left his father to meet his friends. He looked for them at their homes and everywhere, but he couldn't find them anywhere. Then he thought that they might be in their usual meeting place on the hill in the north of the village. It was a bit far, but he ran fast and reached there after some minutes. They were there. Bob and David were speaking with each other and they didn't notice Teddy. He seized the opportunity, got nearer to them, and suddenly, shouted in a very loud and sudden voice "Hi!" Bob and David were scared to death. They stood up and ran after Teddy. They all ran after each other for minutes and each one sat in a side out of breath.

"Should you always do such bad jokes?" shouted Bob panting.

"You were completely immersed in speaking with each other exactly like philosophers, and I thought that it would be good to stop your discussion and tell you a very good news." said Teddy and laughed.

"You, boob!" said David in an angry voice.

"What is your news?" asked Bob.

"Yes! I have a very surprising news that I am sure both of you would be surprised hearing that." said Teddy.

"If your news is like your joking I would never ever like to hear it." said David.

"No! Edgar … Edgar has sent us a letter. I have just got it today. But I haven't read it yet. I tried to find you and read it together." said Teddy this and took out the letter from his pocket. When his friends heard this news, they ran toward him. They were all very happy. It seemed that they all had missed Edgar too much. Then, Teddy opened the letter and started to read it excitedly;

Dear Bob, Teddy, and David,

I hope you are all fine. I have really missed you, my dear friends. I have a lot to say about here, but the letter does not serve me enough. I wake up early in the morning and work until noon. After lunch, I have to learn computer with a trainer called Stephen. It's a bit preachy, but I love it.

I'm experiencing a different lifestyle here beside my new boss, Mr. Thomas. He is very kind and I have spoken about all of you to him and he loves to see you, too. Since I've been here, I have learnt some about computers. That's very interesting and enjoyable. I love to see you again soon. I will write to you more in my next letters. My sweat and dreamy days with you would never be forgotten. It was you who broke my solitude. I will be waiting for your letters. With love. Edgar.

Teddy had finished the letter, but his friends were still silent. It seemed when they read the letter, they missed Edgar more than ever before because after reading the letter, all of them become silent and steeped in dreaming. David was playing with his latchet, sitting on the land.

It was about three o'clock in the afternoon. A large quantity of dark autumn clouds was in the sky of the village with a cold wind. It was about to rain. All the trees were completely out of leaves and there was not any trace of green, but yellow, orange, and barely red. Bob shook his hat on his head and said, "I am very happy that Edgar is experiencing a new lifestyle that is good for him and his future. I am sure that he would be a big computer engineer because he is always sedulous in his life and he would achieve whatever he wants. I wish I were beside him, now."

The rain started and they couldn't sit there anymore.

On other side of the village, in a big wooden house that was covered by bare trees, Sara was beside her mother in the living room close to the fire place reading Edgar's letter to her. She loved to read the letter more and more and, of course, her mother listened to her, carefully. She read all the words of the letter one by one and without any haste. Every word she read had lots of meanings for her. When she finished reading the letter, she loved to find another person to read it for. Ergo, when her father came back from work, she immediately ran toward him, sat on the sofa, and started reading the letter for him. She again read the letter carefully word by word, and Mr. White listened wisely to her. When it finished, she jumped in front of his father and said; "How was the letter dad?"

"It was good; it seems that everything is okay for him there. I was sure that Edgar would satisfy my old friend. Edgar is very polite, and most importantly, he is a very hardworking boy. I see a very clear and successful future for him working there. The last time I was there, Mr. Thomas was very satisfied with him. And also, his progress, in this short time, was very good as his cooperators said to me." Mr. White said.

"Dad! Have you placed any other boy in the shop instead of Edgar?" asked Sara curiously.

"No, my sweetie. I haven't found anyone like him and I don't think I can ever do." said Mr. White and laughed.

"When would he visit us? It has been a long time that we haven't seen him. I've really missed him, dad. I have lots of new paintings that I want to show him" said Sara while he was playing with her dress.

"Next time, when I go to city center for shopping I will take him here if Mr. Thomas accepts. Maybe after two weeks." answered Mr. White wisely and took his daughter's hand and they went to kitchen to have lunch with delicious foods Mary always made.

After lunch, Sara went to her room and picked up a piece of paper and a pen. Then, she started to write back to Edgar. First, she didn't know what to write, but after writing the first line, she was ready and able to write hundred pages. She wrote about herself, her school, village, her parents, her tiny cat, and everything she could write about. Especially, she wrote about her new paintings and explained all of them to him one by one. She wrote about a painting in which many sea birds were flying in the shore under a shining sun; a land covered with spring flowers. When she finished writing, she folded the paper and put it in an envelope.

Next early morning, before going to school, she waited for the mail-carrier in front of their house. She waited for some minutes. Finally, Mr. Richards came and took her letter.

Chapter 6

A young tall man was coming from the end of the corridor with a lot of files and folders in his hands. He was wearing polished black shoes and dark brown striped pants with light brown shirt. He was tall enough even to touch the ceiling. He was putting one foot after another firmly and gracefully. This handsome man was Edgar after about eleven years. Now he was a young gentleman about twenty one years old. He continued his way and entered the office of his manager.

"Hi, sir. I have brought documents you wanted." said Edgar.

"Okay, put them on the table next to the window. Then come and seat beside me." said Mr. Thomas.

Edgar put the documents and folders on the table next to the window and went back beside his boss. He sat down on the sofa, not saying a word. His eyes gazed at the floor as if he was searching something especial there. His beautiful, polite and moral manner and behavior had not been changed; even he had grown up over years. He was exactly the same as his childhood and teenage years; polite, creative, active and even a bit shy. The only thing had been changed was his appearance.

Mr. Thomas looked at him for a while. Then, he went near to the window and drew back the curtain and looked outside for a long time. These weren't strange for Edgar, as he had seen them from his boss several times along these long years he had worked there. After few minutes, Mr. Thomas went back to his seat and turned toward Edgar.

"I don't know how many years I am going to live. Perhaps one day, one weak, one month, and maybe one year or more. I don't know. One day, we are born, and the other day, we die. The length of this journey is short for some people and long for some others. One comes and the other goes even at the moment we are speaking together here in the office. Some people are crying for the loss of their darlings and some other are happy for the birth of a new child at the same time. This circle is going on for many years non-stop and no one could complain about it. Oh, Edgar. I'm sorry; I'm again making you tired by speaking philosophically about life, birth, death and like these." said Mr. Thomas these and took a deep breath.

"No, no, sir. I am always all ears to listen to you. Your advices are always helpful for me." said Edgar this and stared at his eyes as he was waiting to listen to the rest of his speech.

"Thank you, Edgar. You know, you are the only one whom I like to speak to. There is no other one in my life I can speak to about my complexes in life; about what I think I have lost in the past. I always like to think and speak about the philosophy of things, especially life, human beings, and different lifestyles. I don't know what lifestyle is beautiful. Who is auspicious and who is unfortunate.

I have always loved arguing about everything even when I was at primary school. I always asked many strange, surprising, and unusual questions from our teacher. She didn't answer to most of my questions and she always said, "You are too little to know the answers of these questions." By answers like those from my teacher and even my parents, the questions grew bigger and bigger for me day by day, to the extent that I decided to study philosophy in upper levels, but due to some problems I couldn't do that and I studied computer science.

Those small questions which are really big now are still in my mind and I have never found any comprehensive answers for them; and the worse I think nobody could ever find answers to such questions. Many people were born and died without knowing the end of life. I think they just lived in the second of present." Mr. Thomas was completely immersed in speaking and he was depicting all the complexes he had ever had in his life. It seemed he liked to speak for years about the complexes in his life, and he was searching for a fountain to find answers of his questions.

In this moment, his telephone rang and halted him from speaking. When he answered the telephone, he noticed that he was the man who needed the details of the documents Edgar brought him few minutes ago. Edgar put the folders on the table of the boss and left the room by his permission.

When he was closing the door, he saw Mr. Keen near to enter the room. Mr. Keen was the deputy of the company. Mr. Thomas trusted him a lot. He made most of the decisions of the company. But unfortunately, he didn't have good relationship with Edgar even when he was a child and he was new in the company. He never liked Edgar to progress. Edgar himself didn't know what his problem was with him and he always tried to be friends with him, but Mr. Keen never wanted it and always had a very rude manner to Edgar.

After a strange look as usual, they passed each other. Seeing this rude manner from Mr. Keen, again Edgar got sad like always. He loved to be friends with all the people and he would never love to bother anyone. But this guy was very rude to him. He was too sad and so he couldn't get back to his business.

It was about one at noon. He left the work and went outside to walk for a while and calm down. It was nearly the last days of autumn and the weather was very cold. He buttoned up his coat and continued walking.

He went to the park beside the company. He entered the park and walked for a long time. There were many kids playing in the park beside their parents. Tiny girls and boys were playing tag, slide, and whatever they loved. Their parents were a side watching their children kindly and most of the time encouraging them. They mostly laughed and sometimes, they cried when they fell down.

One of the tiny small girls was a good reason for Edgar to go back to long times ago in the past and remember his tiny sister, Lisa. She was dressed in pink and she had long blonde hairs exactly like Lisa. She completely looked like her.

Edgar sat on a wooden bench and watched that girl for a long time while she was playing sweetly. Suddenly, all the atmosphere of the park changed to a hell. He was in the middle of a fire while his parents and Lisa were surrounded him and they were stretching their hands toward

Edgar and begged him to save them. His father was in front of him and his mother on the right and Lisa on the left. He was in dilemma who to save first. He was deep in dreams that a ball hit his leg and took him out of the hell. He looked down and picked up the ball. When he raised up his head, he saw the same girl with pink dress standing silent in front him and just smiling. He gave the ball to her and took a deep breath.

"How terribly I was dreaming!" he thought.

Then, he left that place and continued walking. It was too cold and he fixed his hat and muffler several times not to get cold. There was a big pond in the middle of the park surrounded by tall trees. Some small ducks were swimming in the water. They didn't feel the cold. On the other side, some young boys were throwing small stones into the water. Some other girls were playing with their colorful balloons.

While he was walking, he thought about Mr. Thomas' words about life and death. He could use his advices to perceive and understand his parent's death.

That evening, Edgar was very sad and upset. He didn't know where exactly he was going, but he just wanted to walk and get calm. Sometimes, walking can be the best remedy for a sad person. He felt some strange agitation in his mind with no solution. At this time, he saw a very young boy sitting in a corner in the street. He was very sloppy and untidy and he was wearing some dirty clothes. There was some polishing stuff in front of the boy. That young boy was busy polishing a shoe so hard that he didn't notice Edgar's presence.

Edgar loved the little boy's work and struggle and wondered how serious he was in his job; for an instant, he remembered himself that how hard he used to work when he was a young boy, his age. Edgar looked at his shoes, but they were not that much dirty. However, he asked the young boy to polish his shoes.

The boy turned to him and gave him slippers to wear. Edgar sat beside him on a stool while he was polishing his shoes. He was doing his job as well as he could, without any defect. The weather was very cold and Edgar's fingers were numb, but that small boy was working hard in that hard circumstance without any complaints; even his clothes were not warm enough to keep him warm in that severe cold.

“There must be a reason that this young boy has to work in this circumstance. Otherwise, he could stay at home or at least, he could work in warmer times. No one likes to endure this condition. His coevals are in their warm homes and those outside, are wearing warm clothes and their hands are in their pockets…” thought Edgar to himself looking at that boy. In that moment, the boy coupled his shoes and put them in front of Edgar. He put on his shoes and gave back the slippers. Then, Edgar put his hand in his pocket and took out his wallet.

“Thank you, boy. How much should I pay?” he asked.

“Fifty cents.” answered the boy polishing other shoes.

Edgar found a dollar and gave it to the boy. The boy took it and searched his coins to give back his extra money.

“Don’t. Keep the change. I don’t need it.” said Edgar and smiled kindly to him.

“No, sir. I’m not a beggar. I take money as much as I have to.” replied the boy searching in his coin box.

Edgar was surprised by that answer. He couldn’t believe how serious and gentleman that young boy was! He wanted to make him happy not asking his change, but the boy didn’t like it and ignored his bounty. Edgar really interested in him and wanted to speak to him more, so he asked him slowly, “How old are you, hardworking boy?”

The boy first returned Edgar’s change and when he had closed his small coin box, answered “I am thirteen, sir.” then he continued polishing other shoes.

“I don’t want to interfere in your private life, but can I ask you why do you have to work even in this cold weather?” asked Edgar.

“I work as I have to work because there is no one to work but me. I should earn money; even one dollar a day. It would be enough for me and my old and ill grandmother.” answered the boy while he was working.

"Just one dollar each day? But it is too low." said Edgar this and wondered and pondered for a while. He thought about himself when he was exactly his age. That time he had to work for Mr. White. He didn't have any one to call, to beg, to ask for help or anyone who supports him. But, at least, he had someone like Mr. White to support him and give him a shelter. But this poor boy didn't have any support, and moreover, he had to take care of his old and ill grandmother. Edgar could completely perceive how hard that boy lived because he had passed all that terrible hardships many years ago. He thought he could find a job for that poor boy in Mr. Thomas' company. Since his boss loved him and trusted him, he thought that Mr. Thomas would not deny his request to give a job for this poor boy in the company.

"Would you like to have a much more gainful job?" asked Edgar.

"Beggars can't be choosers. I would like, but there is no job for a young boy like me, except what I am doing right now. I can't do anything but this work." answered the boy desperately.

"But I know a good case for you, boy. Do you know Thomas Computer Company? It's at the end of this street and you can see the last floors of that from here." said Edgar.

"Of course, I know. Who doesn't know that huge company. I sometimes lay my equipments in front of that building as there are a lot of workers and I can polish their shoes." replied the boy.

"I've been working there for many years since I was your age. I started by transferring files and folders from one room to another, but day by day, I learned about computers and now I'm working in a very important part of the company beside the engineers. I actually didn't study academically in any school or university, but I learned computer science with Stephen, one of the master engineers of the company and now, I know everything about computer, even sometimes, more than some original engineers. I will ask my boss to give you a job in the company. He trusts me and I am sure he won't disappoint me. Moreover, you can earn much more money; more than one dollar per day and I will help you as much as I can." said Edgar this and smiled.

"Is it really possible?" replied the boy in full excitement.

"Of course! Now collect your stuff and come with me." said Edgar. Then the young boy collected his polishing equipment rapidly. He was very happy. He collected everything one by one and tastefully and put all of them in his small rectangular metallic box.

Edgar took his hand and they walked toward the company. Now, Edgar felt better after meeting the young boy.

When they entered the building everybody looked at them strangely. They didn't understand why Edgar had taken a polisher boy inside. The young boy couldn't look at anyone; therefore, he fixed his eyes on the floor and just followed Edgar. When Edgar saw this scene he laughed and told the boy not to be shy.

Edgar remembered many years ago when he was a ten-year-old boy and Mr. White took him here to give him a job. Everything was exactly like years ago, but this time, Edgar was not a young boy and he was acting like Mr. White to do good to a person.

They got the elevator and went to the last floor. When they entered the corridor, Edgar saw Mr. Keen coming out of the manager's room. Passing each other, Mr. Keen made a bitter smile to Edgar and left there. Edgar didn't understand him and continued his way and stopped behind door.

"Just stand here, come in when I asked you. Okay?" said Edgar this and winked to him.

"Yes, sir." answered the young boy.

Then Edgar entered the room and greeted Mr. Thomas but he didn't react him well. Edgar was astonished because he always greeted him very well and he had never seen such a cold reaction from him. Mr. Thomas was completely different and he wasn't like always. It seemed that something had happened there. He went beside the window as usual and looked outside, but this time he looked outside too long and didn't say any word to Edgar. He took out a cigarette and smoked it for a while. He was pacing from side to side. He was angry, but Edgar didn't know the reason and he just kept silent in a corner with his hands clasped.

"You are fired, Edgar." shouted Mr. Thomas suddenly.

Edgar got shocked hearing this sentence and became silent for a while and then replied in a small voice "I am fired? But, but why?"

"Don't ask any question. Just leave here. I always spoke to you about the disasters of life. I always complained about life. Go Edgar. Leave here. I want to be alone." said Mr. Thomas, turned to window, and looked outside.

"What have I done wrong, sir?" said Edgar.

"Don't tell anything. I trusted you as my own son; you were the only person I always told my heartaches to. But you abused Edgar. I thought that you are a faithful boy, but I was wrong. Mr. Keen told me everything about you and I can't have you here anymore. You abused the authority I gave to you. Pack your belongings and leave this company soon." said Mr. Thomas and continued smoking.

"I don't understand what you are speaking about, sir. I don't know what the hell that impostor man has told you. But I'm innocent and I have never abused anything. I take oath I have never done. That man doesn't like me since I entered this company. I never could found the reason why he is foe against me!" replied Edgar and his eyes burst into tears.

"Mr. Keen is the man whom I trust first in this company and he had been working for me for over thirty years and he wouldn't ever lie me. There is some shortage in the amount of the products in the part of the company which you are in. and you are condemned to cause this shortage. The amount of shortage is not important for me; your betrayal broke my heart. And Mr. Keen is dependable for me. I don't want to hear anymore and you can go." He said.

"But …" Edgar was left unsaid.

"I said, I do not want hear anything anymore, just leave this company as soon as possible." He stormed.

"Okay, sir. But just I've always been loyal to you and your business and I have never abused anything. I just worked because I had to work and I always obeyed your commands. And this time I will, too, obey you. But one day, it would become clear to you that I was innocent and

Mr. Keen played a trick upon me. Thorns can not be hidden behind beautiful flowers for ever. Bye Mr. Thomas." said Edgar this and left the room while he was very upset and sad because of being condemned for an unpracticed sin. When he entered the corridor, the young boy was sat in a corner. When he saw Edgar he stood up and ran toward him. Edgar cleaned his wet eyes immediately and made a smile not to make him sad. They young boy came closer and stared at Edgar's eyes for seconds.

"Did he accept me, sir?" asked the boy curiously.

Edgar didn't know what to say to that expectant boy and he just said, "Let's go. I will tell you." then they leave there. He went to his room and collected his luggage. When they were going out of the building, Mr. Keen faced them and made a sinister laugh to Edgar and came closer to them.

"You, stupid man. You are a villager and you have to work in a field and plant grain, poor boy. You are not engineer to work here and it was your merit to be fired from this company. Have a good time, man." said Mr. Keen this, laughed, and left. Edgar kept silent and he didn't say anything and went on his way. He was walking in the sidewalk thinking deeply and the young boy was following him.

"What happened sir? You were happy, but after you came out you became sad! I know they didn't accept me because they don't need a polisher in their company. Don't worry for me. I am satisfied with my life and let well enough alone. I think one dollar per day is good for me and my grandmother. I sometimes earn two dollars. Maybe you don't believe, but once I earned four dollars in one day. That day I was really busy, and by the night, I was completely tired, but when I looked at my four dollars I got happy and so did my grandmother." said the boys innocently.

His childlike words were interesting for Edgar. He spoke as if he was the most fortunate person in the world. Edgar didn't know how to answer his words. He wanted to find him a suitable job, but he himself was fired. How strange the life is. Everything can get vice versa in minutes.

"What a strange world it is! I wanted to hire you there, but I was fired. I'm not upset for you because I know you have a beautiful life even with your one dollar per day. I am sad because today some people accused me of an unpracticed sin and I cannot tolerate it. I always did my best to do well and not to do wrong any time. I never expected that, someday, I would face such a bad trouble that happened to me today." said Edgar sadly.

"What would you do now? Where are you going to go?" asked the young boy.

"I have to go to a hotel for some days until I can find a home to rent. I have just enough money to rent a house not to buy. And after that, I have to think what I should do. I have to find a job." replied Edgar.

"I have a suggestion. You can stay with us till you find a place to rent. We are alone and my grandmother would be happy to see you." he said kindly.

"Thank you. You are so kind and generous. Sorry! I have not asked your name, yet." said Edgar

"I'm George, sir" said the young boy.

"And my name is Edgar. You needn't call me sir. Call me Edgar." replied Edgar.

"Okay, Edgar. Now, let's go. My grandmother will be surprised seeing you." said George and pulled Edgar's hand, and they started walking toward his home. They walked for a long time toward southern parts of the city. Passing streets and alleys, the houses were getting older and older and in one of the alleys George stopped and said, "This is our alley and the second house is ours with blue door." The houses around were old, dirty and shattered and their alley was as narrow as just three people could pass beside each other. All the walls around were dirty and humid and full of ridicules shapes on them. They had walked for an hour and half and Edgar was very tired.

"Do you walk this long distance everyday, George?" asked Edgar.

"Yes. I've fallen into the habit of that. It is something like a sport for me." replied George and then he went toward their house and took out his key to open the door. His key was rusty and old, but it worked out. He opened the door, and they entered the house. The sound of the door was like the roaring of a wild animal. It was a very old and dark home, and there were not much furniture around. Edgar sat on the torn sofa and put his suitcase beside it. George went to the next room and greeted his grandmother. She was coughing hard, and it seemed she was very ill. Then George called Edgar to enter the room. When he entered the room he saw an old woman on the bed next to the window. The old woman got very happy seeing the new guest.

"Hi. Please, don't move. It's not good for you." said Edgar.

"Hi. I am okay, son. Feel at home. George told me about you. You can stay here as long as you desire. We are alone here and we don't have anybody to visit us. George and I have been living lonely here for many years." the old woman said hard and coughed again. George brought water and her medicines immediately. Then she felt asleep and they left the room and came to the living room.

They had a small kitchen in a corner of the living room, and there was nothing but an old small refrigerator and gas cooker. Edgar opened the refrigerator and saw nothing but water bottles and some cheese and old woman's medicines. He sighed how poor they were. Then he said to George that he wants to go outside and walk for a while. He came out and searched for a supermarket to buy some things for them as he wanted to live with them, for some days, too. He bought some cheese, butter, milk, meat and different canned foods and too many other things. He came back home with big plastic bags in his hands. When George saw him, he got sad and first he wanted to deny his shopping, but when Edgar said that they were going to live with each other for a while, so he accepted and their refrigerator got adorned and colorful with different foods.

Edgar's cooking was good. Therefore, he started cooking dinner. Each time he wanted to do something, he faced some paucity because they didn't have many stuff in their kitchen. In any case, he made a delicious dinner and they decorated dinner table in George's grandmother's room. That night, George and his grandmother were very happy because they were not alone, and moreover, they were eating a delicious dinner. After dinner, they cleaned the table and washed the dishes together. George's grandmother slept soon, and George wanted to sleep soon, too; he was very tired.

"I want to sleep, don't you?" said George.

"No. I will sleep later. I want to write to one of my friends." answered Edgar.

"Okay. I sleep just here and you can sleep there on the sofa. Good night." said George and closed his eyes.

"Good night, my friend." replied Edgar. Then, he opened his suitcase and took out a pen and a piece of paper. He had in mind to write to Sara as he hadn't written to her for a long time.

"... It has been a long time since I last wrote to you. I received your letter last week and it made me very happy. I was very busy with my work in the company. I liked to be better day by day, but everything finished for me just hours ago. I have very bad news this time. I always wrote to you about my achievements in my job, but this time everything is vice versa. I have been fired out just hours ago without knowing the reason.

A man who always trusted me was against me today. I don't know what was wrong. Just I know that some jealous and wicked men got what they wanted. I am very upset about this matter. I will go there and speak to him again because he should know my innocence.

But I have good news, too. I have found a very good friend. He is thirteen and he reminds me my childhood period. He lives with his old grandmother in a very old and small home. They are very poor, but instead they have very big hearts and I am happy with them. I'll stay here until I found a place to rent.

Please, don't tell about my job to anyone. First, I should prove my innocence to everyone, but I don't know how! I don't know what your father would think about me if he got to know about all this.

Next time, I will write to you my new address. I would like to know what you have done since your last letter. With Loves. Edgar. "

When he finished his letter, it was about midnight, and he felt sleepy. Therefore, he folded the letter, put it in his suitcase and slept on the old sofa. The room wasn't that much comfortable, but some lovely scent had filled the ambience of that small home. Windows were small, but through those small windows, he could see the world much better than ever before. He thought for a long time about George's love to his old and sick grandmother. That small boy worked so hard to earn money to buy his grandmother's medicines and keep her healthy. He had to take care of his old grandmother and he did it very well. But Edgar thought that he couldn't take care of his tiny sister years ago and he lost her thru his own neglect in duty. He blamed himself and he believed that he was blameworthy. He never could forget his neglectfulness. Thinking about these, he closed his eyes and entered the world of dreams.

Next morning, Edgar got up with the sound of the people beyond the window in the street. He woke up and went toward the window and looked outside. There were a large number of people in the street. All were poor and they had worn up dirty and frowsy clothes.

Most of them were factory workers and they had small bags in their hands. They had their work clothes in it while their own clothes didn't differ from their work ones. But they liked to have the gesture of changing their clothes when they enter the work.

Some other young boys like George were in the street, too. They had different kinds of things in their hands. Some had tools in their hands for sale and some other had fabrics. Some of them had flowers most of which were sear, but yet small boys were cheerful to sell them and earn money. They were on their way downtown.

How different the life was in that part of the city. Seeing the people, Edgar started a day with sympathy toward them. He could perceive them deeply because he was one of them when he was young; and maybe worse than them. In one aspect, he loved seeing them because in this way he could remember his past. Memories are always laudable for human being even the bad ones. No one could omit them from his life even if he wants to. All the memories make the whole future.

Edgar turned back and saw no one in the living room. He went to the small room in the corner and saw George giving medicine to his grandmother. They didn't notice him. He came back to small kitchen and washed his face in the colorless sink. The kitchen that was not completely separated from the living room, but it could be called a kitchen. He made tea and breakfast immediately and put them in a tray and went to them.

"Hi grandmother. Hi George. Good morning." he said.

"Oh, dear guest. Come here. I didn't see you well the night before. Come here." the old woman said while she was speaking slowly.

"Good morning, Edgar." replied George and took the glass of water from his grandmother.

"I have prepared breakfast; I hope you enjoy it." said Edgar.

"Thank you, Edgar. But my grandmother doesn't eat breakfast too much. I have just given her medicine." said George.

"Okay. But I like to have breakfast beside your grandmother." Edgar said this and sat beside them. They started having breakfast. When they finished eating breakfast, they went out of that small room to get ready to go out. George had to go to his usual work and do his job and Edgar had to look for a place to rent and maybe a new job. But Edgar still was hopeful to go back to his work beside Mr. Thomas. He believed going back after a couple of days would lead him to speak to his boss and clarify everything to prove his innocence. When Edgar opened his suitcase, a small shiny stone fell and lay on the floor. It was Lisa's stone and it was still shiny and beautiful after years. When George noticed the stone, he wondered about its brilliance.

"How beautiful this stone is!" said George surprisingly.

"Yes, it is beautiful, but it is not that valuable that you imagine. But for me it is very valuable. I bought it many years ago for just three dollars to give it to someone whom I never saw again. And after that day, I've always kept this with me. I believe that it would bring a good luck for me one day." replied Edgar and took the stone from floor.

"But such a shiny and beautiful stone cannot be worthless. I know someone who knows about stones very well. She can help us to know the value of this stone. I'm sure that it's not worthless." answered George.

"Who is she who knows about stones?" asked Edgar.

"She is in the next room; my grandmother. She knows stones very well." said George this and they went to his grandmother. She was staring at the sky from the window beside her bed. She was too old and sick, but a beautiful and kind smile was always on her wizen lips.

When they entered the room, she turned toward them and smiled more. George took the shiny stone from Edgar and gave to his grandmother. She opened her fist and took the stone. She could hardly hold it as her hands were trembling.

"This is Edgar's stone, grandmother. He doesn't know anything about it. He has bought it more than ten years ago, but it's still shiny. I thought that you can tell him what kind of stone this is." said George.

His grandmother looked at the stone for a long time under the light of the sun entering thru the window. Her eyes had been very weak and she hardly could see it. She rotated the stone in her hand and watched all sides of that carefully. Then she looked at them and said, "This is a kind of diamond called Gally-diomond." Edgar and George got shocked by hearing the word of diamond. Then grandmother continued, "This kind of diamond is often found in Gally Mountain, but it is very scarce and rare. That mountain is a volcano; therefore, no one has ever made effort to find diamonds there. But, I've heard from elderly that when that volcano erupts some of this diamonds fall in to the river below the mountain. How did you get this?"

Edgar was garbled. He knew the Gally Mountain very well. It was exactly the name of the volcano which once erupted and took all his family away from him. But it seemed that the volcano had given him a precious diamond.

"I got it in a chance. Years ago, when I was passing an alley in the village next to the Gally Mountain, I saw some boys gathered at a corner. I went closer and saw that one of them had found a stone and wanted to sell that. I had three dollars that day and my sister's birthday was some days later. when I saw the stone I found it beautiful and thought that it would be a good present for my sister's birthday; unlike the boys who thought that this stone is worthless and I am crazy to buy it. Even all of them laughed at me that day. But unfortunately, I never could find the one whom I wanted to give this stone to and I kept it all this long time. This is the story of this stone." said Edgar.

"Now by telling the story, I am sure that this is not a worthless stone and surely it is a priceless diamond. It is very scarce. You are very lucky to have it." The old woman said.

Hearing these words from the old lady, Edgar and George got surprised. They couldn't believe the strange story of the stone. Long years, Edgar looked at that stone as a worthless one and just kept it because it reminded Lisa while he had had a precious treasure.

It was like the story of people who have precious belongings and friends beside them in their life, but they never perceive them.

George was looking at Edgar and the diamond. There was a big treasure and wealth in his hands. The diamond was the size of his small finger and it meant that now Edgar was one of the richest men in the area.

"What would you do with this treasure?" asked George curiously.

"I am really confused and shocked and I cannot believe the strange story of this stone which I should call diamond any longer." said Edgar. Then he continued in a very small voice, "We should show it to jeweler to make sure that it is a diamond. What do you think?"

"I do agree." replied George.

"So, let's go. Today, we are going to ensure that this is a diamond. You won't go to your work and I won't go to find a house for rent. If it is a real diamond, you don't have to polish other's shoes in the cold weather." replied Edgar and smiled. He was thinking about helping many poor people with its money.

"Wow … it would be wonderful." George got surprised first, but then he continued in small voice, "But I love my work even in cold weather. I'm used to my work and my life with my old and sick grandmother in this small home. I love her and she is the only one I have. I would do everything to keep her healthy." His words were very lovely to Edgar. He was a young boy, but his attitude to life was very strange.

They put on their clothes and went out. It was very cold; colder than ever. There was not any jewelry on that area because in that part of the city nobody could buy precious jewels. They even didn't have money to spend their usual life and get by. They were poor and they even didn't have the right to think about the precious jewels. But also it was all the same to them whether to have jewels or not because they never had seen such things except on TV. The worse, most of them didn't have any television to see what they didn't have. Who would crave something that he had never seen and feel before? Maybe that was more comfortable because they never felt the lack of having those things. What they needed was some money to make their ends meet end keep them alive. They wanted to be alive not to live leisurely. Life had a different meaning to them.

Edgar and his young friend went to jewelry in the part of the city where well-off people lived. They stood up in front of a shop's window and stared at the precious stones and other valuable jewels. Their brilliance was like a keen and shiny knife that cleaved the eyesight of watchers. Some of them were light blue and some other was dark red. There were also colors of purple, green and yellow. All were shiny and brilliant.

They entered the shop. It was a very big jewelry with too many workers behind the shop boards. All they were well-dressed. Some rich men were in the shop and their wives were testing different kinds of jewels on their hands, ears, necks and even some of them were testing jewels on their ankle. The numbers of money that were exchanging in their speeches were more than ten, hundred, and thousand and even millions.

One of the workers came toward them and looked at Edgar and George. Edgar was well-dressed, gallant and well-seeming and his being there was not strange for the worker. But George was not well-dressed and his clothes were old and dirty. Exactly like the clothes of people who live in poverty. The worker greeted Edgar, but not much George.

"Can I help you, sir?" said the worker.

"Of course. I have a precious stone and I want to sell it." replied Edgar. Then the worker guided him to one of his colleagues. They went to him and showed the stone to the other worker. The man took the stone from Edgar and looked at it carefully. It took a long time. He examined the stone with different tools and in different ways. He wanted to say something, but he was not sure. It seemed that he had never seen such an alien stone. He looked at Edgar and again at the stone. He was confused. After while, he said, "I have to show it to my boss, he knows about these stones better than me. Let's go upstairs to the office." He said this and they went to his boss's office.

The office was splendid and it was decorated with precious furniture. An old plump man was sitting behind his big work desk. He was playing with the tip of his moustache. He looked strangely at Edgar and especially George when they entered the office. Maybe he didn't expect that one day a boy like George would enter his office. He didn't even offer them to sit. Then he asked his worker, "What do they want here?" His worker without saying any word went near to his boss and gave the stone to him. Then, he whispered very slowly. His boss moved his hand meaning that he could leave the office. The worker went out and closed the door.

George was silent and stood exactly beside Edgar and he was a bit frightened of that fat man's manner. The boss looked at the stone and examined that with his special tools. He did it time and again. Finally, he raised his head up and called Edgar and asked him, "How did you get this stone?"

"I have bought it, sir." replied Edgar confidently and calmly.

The man answered surprisingly, "How did you buy …" But he cut his voice, kept silent, and changed his words. It seemed he wanted to ask something, but he changed his mind. He again looked at the stone. When he looked at the stone, his gesture changed. But he tried to keep his normal gesture and conceal his surprise.

He again played with his moustache and this time smiled and said, "Look, man! This stone is worthless and it's of no value. It is not of those precious stones that you think. But its appearance is beautiful." He looked at George in the corner of the office and said mercifully, "Maybe that young poor boy has found it while hanging out. I can pay you ten dollars and keep this stone just for its shiny appearance. If not it is a shoddy and worthless stone. And I don't need it at all." And he put the stone in front of the Edgar on the desk.

Edgar didn't like the way he spoke, especially when he called George a poor boy. He took the stone and said seriously, "Thank you, sir. If it values just ten dollars I would keep it for myself. As well, that boy is not poor." Then he turned to go.

The man stood up and said, "I didn't want to disturb you. Okay! I'll pay twenty five dollars. Just to keep you satisfied!" Then, he looked at Edgar like the kindest man in the world. Edgar turned to him and said, "How would you offer twenty five dollars for this worthless stone. I want to keep it and I don't want to sell it any more even if you pay a hundred dollars for it."

The man got shocked by Edgar's serious respond. When they were leaving the room he called them again and this time he offered them to sit. Edgar took George's hand and they sat on the sofa. The jeweler went back to his seat and he behaved very generously to them. It seemed that he didn't want to lose that stone.

"I want to be truthful to you. This stone values more, but not as much as you think. And the only one who can buy this stone from you is me. Because no other one knows this stone and no one would pay you more than fifty dollars. Now, when I tell you the exact value of this stone I am sure you would wonder. This stone values about ten thousand dollars and I will pay you eight thousand dollars. And two thousand dollars for me! Is that okay?" the man said while he was smiling.

Hearing that amount of money, George got shocked and he couldn't believe it. He had to polish people's shoes at least for twenty years to save such big money. But Edgar was still calm and serene. He didn't even get surprised. The jeweler expected Edgar to be surprised, but he didn't even smile. The man was completely confused and he didn't know what was passing in Edgar's mind. The fat man could understand that Edgar was not likely to be simple-minded person.

Suddenly, Edgar stood up and said in a loud voice, "You and I both know that this values much more. We cannot deal with each other, sir. You want to defraud us." When he said this, the man's mien got red, became very angry and showed his own face. He was to kill them.

"What do you imagine? I offered you the utmost price that can be offered for this stone. But as I enlarged my offer, you got wrong, and you think that this stone values more than this prices. I don't want this anymore. You can have it for you. Get out of my room." the man shouted angrily and banged his fist on the table.

Edgar took George's hand and they left the room. In the corridor, George turned to Edgar and said curiously, "Why didn't you accept his offer. It was eight thousand dollars. You could do many things with that money."

Edgar smiled and said, "This man was deceitful. Your grandmother said that this is not a stone, but it is a diamond. So, a diamond in this size values more than ten thousand dollars. We would show it somewhere else. Don't worry, boy. This rude man wanted to defraud us."

They laughed and went down stairs. When they were about to open the exit door a man called them loudly from the end of shop, "Don't go. Wait. Wait! Please!" All the costumers turned back and saw a fat man hasty. All of them were surprised of his behavior. His face had turned red and was wet. He was as fat as he couldn't walk accurately. When he saw that all the people were watching him he got ashamed and his forehead got wet more. Nonetheless, he didn't pay any attention to others and went toward Edgar.

"I'm sorry! I got angry. I couldn't control myself. We can deal again. Just come back to my office." The man said and looked at Edgar's eyes exactly like a beggar. What could be the reason that such a rich man was begging Edgar and even George! Edgar was clever enough to know his thoughts. He looked at him wisely and said, "I would come back to your office in one case!"

"Okay! What? I would accept whatever you demand." the man answered hurriedly.

"I would be there just if you accept that this is not a worthless stone, but this is a precious diamond." replied Edgar confidently.

When he said this, the jeweler got shocked and silent. He didn't know what to say. He scratched his chin and said in a very small voice as no one else could hear, "You are right. We can talk about it in my office."

By this sentence, Edgar got satisfied and went back to his office. When they sat in the office, the fat man ordered coffee for them and he made a fake smile on his lips. He tried to act wisely because he had determined that Edgar was a very clever and keen man.

"You are right. This is diamond. I want to be truthful with you this time. I don't want to lose it. But I want to make it a condition. I would tell you the exact value of this diamond, a price that you could never even imagine, if you accept to share it with me. Half for me and half for you ... do you agree?" said the jeweler.

Edgar thought for a while and then said, "I would, if I feel that you are telling the exact price of this diamond."

"I ensure you that you will agree with me when I tell you the dramatic value of this diamond." He smiled and continued, "I have been working in this occupation for more than forty years, but I haven't seen such a big diamond before. This is the biggest one I have ever seen. And also, it is a very scarce diamond that is only found around one of the nearby villages, once in a long time.

The last one that had been found was a smaller one and it had been found about sixty years ago. I just have seen its picture. Now, it is in your hands and even with the half of this diamond's money you would be one of the millionaires of the city." He took a strange look at them and continued in a very small voice, "Such a big diamond would value more than thirty million dollars. Since you promised, half for me and half for you. I would pay you fifteen million dollars." he said this and smiled …

Hearing that amount of money, both Edgar and George got completely shocked. George was looking speechlessly at Edgar. It seemed that he hadn't ever heard the number of million. Edgar was puzzled not only for the number that he had heard, but also for the destiny which he was challenging with. He remembered the day which he bought the stone from those stupid boys. He remembered that day all of them laughed and scoffed at him. What would they do if they had known the value of the stone that day! But all of these incidents were to complete the destiny of the diamond that now was in Edgar's hand. He was immersed in thinking about those days that the fat man broke the silence and said, "What are you thinking about? Do you agree or not?"

"Sorry. I do …" replied Edgar.

Chapter 7

Edgar got a very rich man. Expert enough in computer, soon after taking the money, he founded a computer company. His business grew up day in day out and after two years his company became one of the biggest computer companies in the area.

The bases of his company were on honesty and loyalty. He had a lot of employees in his company and one of them was George. George was the second copy of Edgar in character. Edgar could remember all his past life seeing George. Earning money, Edgar helped many poor people whom he had seen before in George's neighborhood. One of them was George's grandmother. He took her to the best nursing homes and hospitals and so she became healthier and healthier day after day. Money couldn't feed Edgar's mind, but seeing people happy fed his mind very well. He was always the last one to leave the company in the evening and the first to go in the following morning. He earned money to spend in the ways that fed his behaviors in contrary to those who earned money just to save it. Everything was okay in his life and business. The only thing he wanted to do was to go to Mr. Thomas and see him. He didn't have any time during these two years to visit him as he was busy with his company's affairs.

One Monday evening, he left his office and went toward Mr. Thomas's company. When he entered the company and went to his office, he was about to leave there. He was locking his door. As the moment of his turn, he saw Edgar. It was just two years that they hadn't seen each other, but Edgar's prior boss had grown older. He had changed completely. He had got slim and pale in face. When he saw Edgar, he looked so strange as if he had been waiting for him with all his heart.

They both burst into tears and hugged each other warmly and firmly. Mr. Thomas embraced Edgar firmly though with his trembling hands. He turned back, unlocked the door, and they went inside. It was getting darker and composedly sun and moon were changing their places as they did it since the beginning, and stars were appearing in the sky of the town. All the employees had left the company except the door keepers. The whole building was in utter silence.

Edgar and his prior boss stared at each other for a long time without saying a word. They were speaking to each other thru their eyes; sometimes eyes say words that tongue could never explain. Mr. Thomas broke the silence and said, "Where were you, dear Edgar? One month after that sinister event, I looked for you wherever I could …"

"Nowhere special. Since my childhood, my life was full of unexpected incidents that have always changed my lifestyle. And I have always got along with them. The last incident I experienced was the most unbelievable one which again changed the style of my life completely. I would require a long time to explain it." replied Edgar and sighed deeply.

"My dear Edgar! I know you; even better than myself. I know how wise and flexible you are to put up with any incident and change in your life. You even responded my fault with a meaningful silence that time, but I couldn't understand it. One month after I fired you, I understood you were innocent as usual, but it was too late and you were not here. The man who had stolen the products of the company came to me and confessed everything. He said that it was Mr. Keen's trick practiced thru him. Mr. Keen had promised the man to share the stolen goods with him, but he did not do that, and therefore, that employee came to me and explained everything. That day, I was sad for two things. First, how sinister Mr. Keen could be to me; the one whom I trusted those long years. And second and more important, was that I had lost you and impulsively accused you of stealing. Contrite, I looked for you days and months, but it was no use and I couldn't find you anywhere. All this time, I have lived just as a guilty person who accused an innocent man. When I fired Mr. Keen and lost you, there was no one I could trust in this company and I didn't know how I managed it." said Mr. Thomas while his eyes were wet.

"You must not be sorry because I have never been disturbed by you. I owe all my life to two people and I would never forget them. The first one is the man who saved my life and looked after me as his own son. And always took care of me even in the hardest situations. He is no one except Mr. White. And the second one is who accepted an illiterate young boy in his big and modern company and taught him everything. He is the man who is sitting in front of me now. He is you, Mr. Thomas. I always owe you sir. And now I just wanted to tell you about my innocence again because I believe that time can heal the pains. But fortunately, you yourself have known everything. Good and evil have shown themselves to you. It was the only thing that I believed that you would know the truth one day." said Edgar and smiled.

"You are as kind and wise as usual. If you didn't come to see me, I would never forgive myself. Now, I got better knowing that you have forgiven me. But I am getting older and older everyday. A year after losing you, I lost my wife, too. Poor woman had a brain stroke. She was in hospital for a month, but finally, doctors dashed my hope and she died in front my eyes. I couldn't do anything for her. I spent thousands of dollars, but money couldn't save her; the money which I spent all my youth and life to earn it. But it couldn't save my wife's life." he said this and burst into tears.

"God bless her. I got very sorry to hear this." replied Edgar in a very small voice.

"During that one month, I felt how cruel I was to my wife. I spent all my time to earn money and I thought that I was doing it for my love and my family. But I was in a wrong way. It was not the right way. After her brain stroke, she was on the bed of the hospital and the only thing she could do was to look. She could only look at me. She couldn't tell any words. She couldn't move her head or hands. She was just looking innocently. But instead, I talked to her too much. I confessed her all my faults and I told her how much I loved her. I explained how we met each other, how we married, how we passed the first years of our common life. But the last day, she couldn't look at me anymore. She closed her eyes and never opened them again. And now, I was going to her grave to requiem her as everyday I go. I go to the church yard and speak to her gravestone for many hours. I won everything and then lost all of them without knowing their value …" he said.

"I see. And I sympathize with you. Losing some one whom we love is very hard. But we have to accept it and be patient." replied Edgar.

"Your presence here makes me feel better. What do you do now? Where did you go when you left here? Where are you now?" asked Mr. Thomas. When he asked this question, Edgar told him the whole story. He told him about George and his kind grandmother. He said that he had founded a computer company. He told his company's name; Diamond. When Mr. Thomas heard his company's name, he got surprised.

"Oh, my God! Diamond Computer Company is yours! I hear its name many times these days. It has become a very famous company. And now I am very happy that it's yours. You deserve more than these. But I advise you not to repeat what I did. Never sacrifice your life to money. Also, I am sure you are wise enough not to do such things." he said.

"Thank you, sir. All I have belongs to you because you taught me everything." replied Edgar humbly.

"No, boy! You yourself deserve all these things. I am really tired of this city and working in this company. I think now I am too old to work. I want to go back to the country. I have a big farm beside my friend's; Mr. White. I will go there and live the rest of my life there. That would be better for an old man like me. Living beside the trees and flowers would be fabulous. I can get up early every morning and go to barns and feed the animals. Then, wash my face in the cold water of the river down my farm. I think they would be better for me than working here in the city; under this polluted sky.

Counting numbers are hard and boring for me now. I am too old to give them commands. I cannot ask about problems. I am not eager to produce a new product and race my rivals in the market. I have had enough of that. Once, I decided to go to country, but I couldn't as I was worried about the future of this company. I don't need this company and all its assets and I could leave here even without telling anyone. But I was worried about people who are now working here and I couldn't find any one to manage the company after me. I needed a person who could manage the company well enough; not firing present employees, but also employing new ones." he looked at Edgar, smiled, and continued, "But now, I can go wherever I wish because I have found the person who can manage here. That man is you, Edgar."

By telling this, Edgar got shocked. Then he said, "I am always at your service. But you know that I am busy with my company, and more importantly, your company is very big and I am not capable to control it. You always count on me more than I deserve."

"No. I trust you well enough. And I know how hardworking you are in your affairs. You should do it if you want to help me. Do you accept it?" said Mr. Thomas.

"I can never disagree with you." replied Edgar.

When he accepted it, Mr. Thomas got happy and wrinkles on his forehead and lips got a bit strained. By this time, Edgar faced a new burden which was very important. He had to take over control of the biggest computer company in the area; this was besides handling his own which was not that smaller than that of Mr. Thomas.

After speaking for a long time, they left the company. Mr. Thomas wanted to go to his wife's grave and Edgar respectfully accepted. They went there at about night. They didn't drive and wended the whole path walking. Mr. Thomas talked so long to Edgar as he hadn't talked to anyone for a long time because there wasn't anyone to talk to.

They reached the graveyard in utter darkness of the night. Only some globe lamps had lighted there. They found the grave of Mrs. Thomas which was in a corner under an old locus tree. When Mr. Thomas sat beside her grave, his eyes burst into tears without lapse of time. Edgar sat beside him and took his hand around his shoulders and pushed him. The old man was murmuring some words very slowly and pushed his hand on the grave. Then, he took out a small bottle of perfume and opened it and rubbed some of that on the grave, "She loved this perfume very much and everyday used it. For this reason, after her death, I bring this perfume here every night and rub on her grave." He said this and stood up. They left there and went toward the gate.

"Would you come with me to my house now? I am really alone. There is no one in my house except two servants. They are kind and loyal to me, but they are not whom I can speak to." said Mr. Thomas.

"I really loved to … but if I come with you, George and grandmother would be worried. Also, they are worried now. I will come to visit you early in the morning, tomorrow." replied Edgar.

"You sure do it. Good night." said the old man and wore his brown hat. He then disappeared in the darkness of the night. Edgar watched him go afar immersed in thinking about him. George reminded Edgar of his childhood and this old man visualized Edgar's old ages. He was in the middle of the life road; George was behind him, and Mr. Thomas in front of him. He would never be George again, but one day, he would be as old as Mr. Thomas. A cold rain drop distracted him and brought him to the world; he turned and went toward his house in which he lived with George and his old grandmother. When he reached home, it was a bout eleven o'clock. Grandmother had slept, but George was still awake.

"Hi, George. You always sleep sooner than this, but you are still awake!" said Edgar while he was taking off his coat.

"I was waiting for you …. You were late and I got worried." replied George.

"I'm sorry. As I told you, I went to visit my prior boss. It took a bit long. Poor man had grown so old. He spoke too long to me, and then we went to his wife's grave," Edgar came to breath, "because of that I came late. How is grandmother?" asked Edgar.

"She is fine. She is getting better everyday. She doesn't cough any more. She just slept an hour ago." replied George.

"Okay! You can go and sleep. It seems you are very sleepy. I am very tired, too. Good night." said Edgar in small voice and went to his bedroom. They had moved to a new house in the better part of the city. It was bigger than the previous one and all of them had their own separate room.

Next morning, Edgar went to visit Mr. Thomas. It was about 8 o'clock in the morning. All people were going to work and some of them were opening their small and big shops. The butcher was hanging fresh meat on the hook in front of the shop. The confectioner was turning on his ovens to make delicious sweets. Peddlers were trying to sell their things every here and there. Some of them were old and some others very young. All of them were starting their days in hope of earning money and having a good business day.

In the entrance of the company, Edgar saw the doorman who was middle-aged and a very kind man. He got very happy seeing Edgar as he loved him very much. Not only the doorman, but also all of the employees of the company loved him and did respect him. The only one who was not good to him was Mr. Keen who smarted for his wrong behavior. He tried to spoil Edgar, but finally he had spoiled himself and it's the end of people who want to play tricks on others.

Walking in the corridor, Edgar took a look at his watch and thought that he was a bit soon. "Mr. Thomas couldn't have came yet." he thought; but the office door was open and when he entered inside, he saw Mr. Thomas sitting on his seat.

"Hello. Good morning, sir." said Edgar wearing a smile on his face.

"Good morning, dear Edgar. I was waiting for you. Look at that table on the corner. There are some files and folders on it. They are all you would need to know about the company. Read all of them carefully and start your work as soon as possible. From now on, you are the one who decides in this company. I am leaving here just today. I called Mr. White last night. Alas, he was sick and he could not speak well. I think I had better go beside him. We are old friends and we know each other very well." said Mr. Thomas.

"I assure you that I would read all these files carefully and I would do my best to control here in your absence." replied Edgar.

"Thank you. You always make me happy." came the answer.

"But I got worried about Mr. White. Is he very sick?" asked Edgar curiously.

"Neither good nor bad. But he had difficulty speaking." answered Mr. Thomas.

"Poor man! I haven't seen him and his family for a long time. I have really missed them. I can drive you there. So, I can visit hem. But just if you accept." Edgar replied saying the last words in doubt of being accepted.

"How can I deny your kind suggestion? All willingly, I do agree. I have to do some small stuff by noon. I will be waiting for you at home, at 2 o'clock." said Mr. Thomas happily.

Jolly to overpass his doubt, Edgar said, "Okay. I would be on time." He then left there and went to his own company to do his affairs. Then, he called George and told him that he was going on a short trip. Around noon, he packed his suitcase and went to take Mr. Thomas to village. On the way, he stopped at a big store and bought some gifts and souvenirs for Sara and others. Earlier years, when he wanted to go to the village, Edgar bought dolls and similar things for Sara, but now she was already a young girl, and this time, Edgar bought her a beautiful dress. Then, he went to Mr. Thomas's home, took him, and drove toward the village.

It was a shiny day. By getting far from the city, the sky got clearer and clearer. It was the first of May and everywhere was green, fresh, and vivacious. Mr. Thomas was as happy as a prisoner out of prison. He looked at green hills, colorful flowers, and tall trees; he felt calm and serene. He smelled all fragrant scents around himself with all his might. He listened carefully to the birds singing beautifully on the branches of the trees. Apparently, the beauty of nature outperformed the sound of car engine; Mr. Thomas did not seem to be distracted with it at all. He was totally immersed in it.

"How beautiful the nature is! I think all the things around me are speaking to me and they are greeting me with all their hearts. Hills, birds, flowers, trees, sky, but I don't know how to respond to them. Their language is completely different from mine. They speak kindly, innocently, and honestly. In my mind, we can never respond to them the way they deserve, but they still smile to us."

"You are right. Life in the nature is really something. And I think the secret of this beauty is its simplicity. I mean simplicity has decorated their lives in a simple style and because of that they are always new and they never get boring in eyes." said Edgar with a smile admiring the beautiful nature.

After some hours, they reached the village. It was all green. The sky was bluer than they could imagine. Edgar stopped on the bridge which connected the road to the entrance of the village. It was an old bridge crossing a wide river. He got off the car and stared at the village. It was a long time since the day when he had left there for the first time to continue his life in the city. After that year, he had visited the village just twice and it was when he was a young boy. Now after years, he had gone to a place that all parts of that were full of good and bad memories for him. How could he forget those memories; even the bad ones? No one can delete the memories from his mind. Memories are some of the radical elements of the brain. Those who think they have forgotten their memories are in a big fault.

Mr. Thomas, too, got off the car. He went beside Edgar and stood for some time looking directly at the village. He sure had memories, too.

"I left here when I was a child. I was about seven. Mr. White was my best friend. We were close friends. When my father decided to move from village, we both got very sad. We always played with each other and there wasn't a day we didn't meet. When we left here, my parents promised that I and Mr. White would meet each other every week. My father loved hunting. He came here to hunt and so I had an opportunity to see my friend. You know," Mr. Thomas said with an air of no name toward his friend and went on, "when his father came to city to buy goods, he came with Mr. White and we could see each other more and more. I went to school and continued my studies until I graduated from university in computer engineering. But he didn't study and worked beside his uncle from his childhood. Those were the days! Now, we are two old men and tired of life. We are passing days to join the sky." said Mr. Thomas sighing deeply.

Edgar could not take it in, so asked, "I have always wondered how a good and stable friendship you have! You have never lost it even in times of separation." said Edgar while looking at the old man; maybe he tried to learn the secret of this friendship.

"Yes, we have always been in touch. Sometimes, some evil-eyed people tried to make us drift apart, but we never paid attention to the gossips. And more importantly, we put up with each other very well. These are the secrets of our friendship that have kept us friends since old days." Then, he smelled the fresh air of the village.

While they were talking to each other and enjoying the beautiful view of the village, a young man passed there. He was going to the village. He was a tall boy with black hair. He looked serious, but kind. He was wearing a suit and a red tie. He seemed wise and he was walking gently through the wayside. He had a brown bag in his hand and shook it back and forth calmly. When Edgar turned back to get in the car, he noticed that young man. Edgar took a profound look at the young man as if he knew him from somewhere. But he couldn't get to know him. At that moment, the young man looked at Edgar, too. They got closer and again looked at each other.

"Good evening. Are you new comers here?" asked the passerby kindly.

"Good evening. Not that much new, but now, we can be called new." replied Edgar.

"I didn't get you!" said the passerby and he was surprised.

"I mean once we lived here. But it is a long time that we have been far away from here; that is more about my friend, Mr. Thomas." came the answer.

Mr. Thomas became closer and stood beside them. Then, he said, "Now, when I stand here, I feel newer than everyone. I just passed my childhood in this heaven. But I had to live the rest of my life in that hellish city."

"So, if one day you lived here I have to know you. I have been living here all my life. Only, I left here to continue my studies; just for about four years. When I finished my studies and became a teacher, I came back here as soon as possible. I could never resist being far from here. As you said, here is like a heaven and everyone loves to be in the heaven. Excuse me! Can I ask your name?" said the teacher and smiled.

"Of course. This is Mr. Thomas and my name is Edgar." replied Edgar.

Hearing their names, the passerby kept silent. He didn't say any words and just kept looking at Edgar. It seemed his eyes were going to burst into tears. Such a strange reaction from the young man made Edgar wonder.

"Sorry, but are you okay? Did I say anything offensive?" asked Edgar wonderingly.

"No … no. I am fine. I'm better than I could ever be. You are Edgar, my best friend. This is me … I am Bob …." answered Bob happily. Hearing this, Edgar got surprised and they hugged each other warmly as they didn't want to separate. Drops of tear wetted his cheek when Mr. Thomas saw this scene.

They all got in the car and drove inside the village. Edgar, first, drove Bob to his home. In that short distance, they spoke as much as they could about everything possible. Even seconds were full of words between them.

"I can feel how happy your parents are now. I remember they hoped you would be a teacher when you grew up. And now, you are a teacher." said Edgar revealing his vivid memory. They were in front of Bob's house. They loved to speak more and more as they had a lot to talk about the long years they were far away from each other. Edgar dropped Bob and promised him to go to him later.

Finally, they reached Mr. White's house. It had changed a bit. The trees of the garden had grown older like the people of the village and they had surrounded the whole garden and building. Sunshine could hardly touch the ground in their house.

Mr. Thomas got off the car and entered the yard. Edgar was taking out the suitcases from the rear boot of the car. Mr. Thomas rang the bell and waited at the door. After a short while, the door opened and a beautiful girl appeared. She was the prettiest girl he had ever seen.

She had expressive and charming eyes with their beautiful green color. She was wearing a long dress in pink. And her hair was adorably long. It was Sara who had grown up. She had become a mature girl and her body was like paring Paris doll.

"Good evening. Is it Mr. White's home?" asked Mr. Thomas.

"Yes, can I help you?" answered Sara vivaciously. She didn't remember Mr. Thomas as she had not seen him for a long time. The last time Mr. Thomas had gone to the village was over fifteen years ago when Sara was a little girl. But she always had heard of Mr. Thomas from his father.

"I'm Thomas, young lady." answered Mr. Thomas.

"Wow, dear Mr. Thomas. Welcome; it is my pleasure to see you, father has always told me about you. I am very happy to see you. My father would be very delighted if he sees you here. Please," Sara gesticulated in, "came in, sir." She was to close the door that Mr. Thomas told he was not alone and then went inside. Sara turned back and looked outside. She couldn't believe her eyes; on the other side of the fence beside the car.

She ran toward the gate and stood there looking at Edgar. She looked so deep as if she had been waiting for that scene for many years. Edgar was not aware of her presence. He closed the doors of the car and came toward home with three big suitcases in his hands. When he saw Sara, Edgar got surprised. That small Sara had become a mature girl and her mien had completely changed.

"Hi, Mr. Oliver. Welcome." said Sara in a sweet and small voice while she had beautiful smile in her lips. She called Edgar with his last name as they were well-grown and they were not the same children who were close friends of each other. She loved him more than before, but she found him a bit strange as they were far away from each other for many years. But the main reason was something else. Maybe she was stressful.

"Hi, dear Sara. How much you have changed! You look better than always. And you have become more beautiful." said Edgar serenely without any stress, but it was clear that he was immersed in her beauty. They walked the garden and went inside. It took a bit long as it seemed that the garden was miles. But the garden was not long as miles; the two were walking slowly. Sara could not keep looking at Edgar even for a second.

When they entered home, the next one who got surprised by seeing Edgar was Mary. She had grown old and her hair was gray. Some wrinkles had decreased her beauty on her face. But her kind manner was still stable. But a deep sadness could be felt in depth of her eyes and it was because of his husband's illness.

Mr. Thomas was not in the hall. He had gone to his friend's room just at the moment of arrival. The three went to Mr. White's room, as well. When they entered the room, they faced a soulful scene. The two old friends were beside each other. They were speaking about everything possible, but mostly, they remembered their funny memories; they could not laugh briskly as they were too old to laugh like young people. They looked at each other's hair and laughed again.

"Your hair is as white as snowballs I would throw at you in winters. One day, they were as black as your pupil." said Mr. Thomas slowly and smiled.

"That's right, but you could never hit me with your snowballs. You were fat and couldn't run as fast as I could. You never lose weight, but get fatter and fa ...." answered Mr. White left unsaid due to coughs.

Mary cut in on the two old men by knocking on the door. They stopped speaking and looked at the door. Edgar went to Mr. White's bed and knelt beside that.

"Hi, Mr. White." said Edgar in a very small voice.

"Oh, Edgar!" Mr. White said ready for later words of surprise, "My dear son. Now, you are really one of the most handsome men in the world. What a beautiful day it is today. I am beside my old friend and my son, Edgar. I had really missed you and now I feel much better." said Mr. White calmly in a small voice.

"I do agree with you, my dear friend. Edgar is the matter of reliance. As a matter of fact, he was the only one I could speak to all these years. I should always be grateful to you to have made him a friend of mine. He is clever, polite, kind, and whatever you could find in an ideal friend."

said Mr. Thomas with eyes fixed on Edgar. Edgar nodded his head and stared at the bed. Mary had left the room, but Sara was still in the entrance. Sara seemed to be all ears when her father and Mr. Thomas were talking about Edgar and his being good.

After speaking for a while, Edgar and Sara left the room and went downstairs, but Mr. Thomas stayed beside his friend. Those two old men had a lot to talk about. When Mr. Thomas explained his plans of living in the village for the rest of his life, Mr. White got very happy as he could be beside his old friend again and he had someone to talk to in times of lonesomeness. They ate their lunch in the room and unexaggeratedly talked until midnight.

Downstairs, Edgar, Sara, and her mother were dinning. After a light supper, Sara and Edgar went upstairs. They, first, went to Edgar's room which was still vacant. Then, they went to Sara's room. All the walls were covered by the fantastic paintings of Sara. Most of them were new and Edgar hadn't seen them before. Sara had become a very professional painter.

"How beautiful paintings you have painted!" uttered Edgar surprisingly.

"Thank you; these are all what I could do. But I remember you painted beautiful pictures, too." said Sara and smiled.

"Yes, but I could never paint as beautiful as yours. I loved to continue painting, but when I left here, I didn't have any opportunity of doing that. I worked all morning till noon. I then would study until night. I got very tired by the end of the day and the only thing I could do at night was to sleep deeply." answered Edgar.

They talked long about such things. It could be perceived that Edgar had some influence on Sara; maybe more than some. But impeccable Sara was the lightest in Edgar's mind. Edgar didn't notice Sara's feelings about him. Maybe poor Sara did not notice it herself in her mind. Maybe she couldn't recognize her feelings about Edgar, but whatever it was, it was something strong. She played a very beautiful music for Edgar with her violin. She played the loveliest songs she had ever played.

Edgar loved her performance very much and clapped him for a long time.

That night passed with all strange emotions between Sara and Edgar. Edgar slept in his room. Mr. Thomas slept beside his friend. Although in habit of sleeping in separate room, this was what Mr. Thomas preferred. All of them slept in the darkness and silence of the night. Some martins in the yard on the walls sang the whole night.

Next day early in the morning, the sun peeped over the horizon and made everywhere light. A special aromatic air had surrounded the whole yard. Small birds were flying in the blue sky. Dogs were barking in the garden. Farmers were going to their fields and the sheepherder was taking sheep to meadows for grazing.

After having breakfast, Edgar got ready to leave the village and go to city to do his work there. He had a lot to do. Two old friends were still beside each other. They ate breakfast together. Mr. White was better than before. Edgar went upstairs and bade Mr. White and Mr. Thomas a farewell.

When Edgar was fixing his car outside, Sara and his mother were beside him standing at the gate. Sara was not happy. She was silent. Edgar finished fixing and turned to them, "Okay! The car is ready now. I have to go."

"You made us very happy. I hope you come again very soon. We are always waiting for you." said Mary.

"Who knows how long it takes him to be back again?" thought Sara to herself and she was sad.

"It was nice seeing you again after all these years. I would come again as soon as possible. Thanks for everything." said Edgar and got in the car. Mary went home, but Sara was still there. When her mother left, Sara went closer to the car, "Have a good trip, Mr. Oliver."

"Thank you. I hope to see you again." replied Edgar and switched on the car. Sara was still looking at him. She was playing with her dress with her slender fingers. She again got closer and said, "But …" and she cut in on herself soon.

“What did you want to say?” asked Edgar.

“Nothing, sir; nothing.” replied Sara precipitately and winced. Then, Edgar gave her a handshake and drove away. Sara went home drenched in deep sadness. It seemed she had a lot to say, but she couldn’t.

Edgar had a charming smile on his lips. He always had it, but this time it emerged more beautifully while driving the car. He was immersed in the nature of the village. He would like to live in the village, like Mr. Thomas, but he couldn’t. He had a lot to do in the city. Suddenly, he got sad and thought that he was sentenced to have the same life. If he always works and gets busy with his job, when can he enjoy the nature? When can he be beside whom he loves? Thinking about such things, he reached where he entered the village the day before.

Suddenly, he saw an old woman and a young girl beside her on one side of the road. They were waiting for a car to go to city. Edgar stopped right away in front of them and said that he could drive them to city. The old woman accepted, and they got in the car.

The old woman was very sick and coughed frequently. The girl beside her had a bag of drugs which surely was the old woman’s. Edgar got disturbed seeing her coughing that hard. He increased his speed and drove faster. Edgar looked at old Woman from rear view mirror. So familiar to him, Edgar couldn’t remember her.

The girl beside her was young and maybe about seventeen. She had hugged the old woman in the backseat. She had very charming eyes and it had taken Edgar’s attention. She had all good features of a young girl; slender body with long neck, long hair, gray eyes, and a well-shaped nose. She was a very pretty girl. If she lived in ancient Greek era, she could be called ATHENA—the goddess of beauty and wisdom. She never looked at Edgar and was dutiful toward the old woman. Passing time, the old lady got worse and she coughed more and more.

Edgar drove faster and they reached the city very soon.

“Thank you, sir. We get off here; we can take a taxi to hospital.” said the young, beautiful girl speaking for the first time. The old woman was still coughing and she could not speak.

"No, she is not good enough. I will drive you to the hospital." replied Edgar and then drove toward hospital. When they reached there, he went along with them to the doctor. He did everything needed. After a while, the old lady got better and stopped coughing.

"Thank you, son. You really did not have to." said the old lady slowly.

"You're welcome. It was my pleasure to help you. Are you okay now?" replied Edgar and smiled.

"Yes, much better. Every three months, I have to come here and visit my doctor. It has been about five months since I was last here; so I was too bad this morning." said the old woman sorry to have neglected the visit.

Suddenly, Edgar made a very strange decision. He said that he had to come back to village and he could drive them back. The old woman accepted. Then, he first drove to his company.

"I will come back soon. Just wait a little." Then, he left them and went to his office. In the corridor, he saw young George.

"Hi, sir. How soon you came back!" said Gorge happily.

"Hi, George. I came soon, but I have to go back to the village. Please, call Mr. Robert right away." urged Edgar. Mr. Robert was a middle-aged man of about forty. He was experienced in management, and of course, he was a computer excerpt. Mr. Robert was also a very honest and trustworthy person. After Edgar, he was the second man in the company and all the employees had to obey him.

Mr. Robert went to office, and Edgar told him that he had to go on a trip for a while and he should take control of the company; also Mr. Thomas's company. Edgar was sure that he could handle it. Mr. Robert was cut out for such situations.

"I will come back as soon as possible." said Edgar and left the office. In the corridor again he saw young George. He was going from one room to another with a lot of files and folders in his hands. Edgar stopped him and said, "I am going. Tomorrow, grandmother should visit the doctor. Don't forget. Take care of everything."

"Sur, sir. We will miss you." replied George.

"I will come back as soon as possible." repeated Edgar emphatically and gave him some money. Then, he left the company and went to his car. The old woman and young girl were still in the car. He got in the car and switched it on.

"I am sorry, I am late." said Edgar and smiled.

"No problem." answered the old lady.

It was about noon. For quite a while, there was a deep silence between them. The most silent person was the young girl who scarcely moved her beautiful and red lips to say a word. She was a bit shy. But something was clear. She loved the old woman a lot. "She is her Grandmother." thought Edgar. Her lips didn't say any words, but instead her eyes were full of words. And it had intensely influenced Edgar. Edgar had the strangest feelings about either the young girl or her grandmother.

In the middle of the path, Edgar stopped at an inn for lunch. It was not a big one, but some things could be found to eat for lunch. In front of the inn, there was a wooden table under the shadow of an old tree. When they sat there, the old land lord came to them and took their order. He was very fat and could almost not move himself. While he was going inside, suddenly, he fell down; it made the young girl laugh. She was more beautiful when she laughed. But when she noticed Edgar looking at her, she stopped laughing and her cheeks got pink.

All her actions had a deep affection on Edgar; even her walking style. He felt very strange. Those were such strange and baffling feelings that he had never experienced before. He couldn't recognize what he was thinking about at that moment. He couldn't be on familiar terms with his feelings, but he knew it was very deep and strong. It was a sort of energy that pushed him toward that young girl. Not only was her appearance charming, but also her actions and conducts were attractive.

After eating lunch, they went to the village and Edgar drove them to their home. He was so watchful not to be seen in the neighborhood because he didn't want others to know his being in the village, chiefly Mr. White's family. The old lady's house was familiar to him. It was a big house. It did not have a big front yard, but it had a big back yard. The design of doors and windows, and the small veranda in front of the house were all familiar to him. By this time, Edgar was completely perplexed. He, swimming in the sea of past, couldn't find any island or seashore to save himself. He still had to swim with all his strength.

"Come in and take a rest, son. You should be tired; you have driven all day long." said the old woman.

"Thank you, madam. I will, but not now. Tomorrow, I will come to see you."

The young girl was still beside her grandmother and Edgar was looking at her even when speaking to the old woman. There were enough clues for such a clever, old lady to get to know why of Edgar's strange behavior. She smiled and went inside to leave them alone. Not only did she not disagree with their speaking, but also she wanted her beautiful granddaughter to speak to such a handsome man. It seemed that the old lady could read Edgar's mind. The elderly always know what is on young people's mind because one day they were young and experienced what the youth are trying now. Edgar left there because he knew that he had to leave sooner or later and he couldn't stay there for good.

He went to an inn to stay there. It was about three miles far from the village. He went there as he didn't want to be seen by others. It was like a deserted inn. "Secure and far from the village." thought Edgar. There lived just a landlady and her daughter; no passengers were there. They got surprised seeing Edgar as if they hadn't seen a person for a long time. Seeing a person was surprising for them especially such a handsome man like Edgar. The landlady was about sixty and she was a bit fat and her daughter seemed to be about twenty. She was thin and graceful and had a normal beauty. She took a key from her mother and guided Edgar upstairs. She showed Edgar a room exactly beside the last stair. She put away the white curtain and made the bed.

"Here is ready, sir. Call me with the bell on that table whenever you need anything." said the girl.

"Thank you. Certainly." replied Edgar. The young girl went toward door to exit, but right at the door, she stopped, turned back, looked at Edgar charmingly, and then left. Her behavior was so strange for Edgar. He put his only small suitcase at a corner and lay down on the bed. It was not that comfortable, but he could get by for some days.

It was about seven o'clock and the sky was getting darker. The sun had disappeared and the stars were emerging little by little. They sky had a beautiful color of dark blue and purple. These two colors combined with each other and it all had made a romantic scene. Again God had shown a drop of his art in creating beauties to his creatures.

After a very short nap, Edgar got up and felt hungry. He went downstairs to the kitchen and saw the landlady cooking. He sat on a chair and drank a glass of water.

"Do you live alone with your daughter?' asked Edgar.

"Yes, I do." answered the landlady in a small voice and went on cooking.

"Sorry if I ask, but why here is so empty and I am the only passenger of your inn?" asked Edgar curiously.

"It has a long story; I have been living alone for a long time with my daughter here which is a house now. Once, this inn was the most famous in the area, but everything changed over a night. Ever since then, we barely meet passengers; as if here is cursed. And I am sure you have not heard of this inn." said the landlady sorrowfully and put the soup pot on the table and set it with three wooden bowls. Her spoons were wooden, too. "We always eat with these wooden cutleries and dishes. These are my daughter's handicrafts; I like them."

"Eating in these should be tasty. Where is your daughter now?" asked Edgar and smiled.

"Her name is Emily. She is busy feeding the cats in the backyard. Her cats are the only guests of our inn and she feeds them every night." answered the landlady and served soup to Edgar. They started eating dinner. Emily was still outside playing with her cats.

"Can I have one more bowl? It was really delicious." requested Edgar.

"Of course!" the landlady exclaimed with a lift in her eyebrows as if stunned of Edgar's words, "It has been so long since last one commented on my food." After finishing dinner, she took out a cigarette from her pocket and put it on her pale lips.

"Do you smoke?" she asked.

"No, thanks. I don't smoke, but if it doesn't matter, I would like to ask you about the story of this inn?"

The landlady lit her cigarette and started smoking. She blew its smoke to ceiling like a captain sitting in his cabin smoking. Then, she looked at Edgar and explained, "It goes ten years back. Here was the most famous inn in the area and everyone came to our inn. And here was not in such a bad situation that you see now. It was clean and many servants worked here.

All rich passengers and merchants stayed in our inn. Here was a secure and comfortable place for them.

We had a gardener. He always kept the yard and garden neat and tidy. Outer face of the inn was attractive for all passengers." She flicked her cigarette in the ashtray and continued, "But an evil incident changed everything. That sinister night darkened my life. That night, the inn was full of passengers. We were busy with serving them.

That night, we had a very important guest. He was one of the richest peoples in the area. He was very famous and well-known. Having a guest like him was a matter of pride, but the following morning, a disaster came up.

He was alone. We prepared him the most comfortable room of the inn with a beautiful view of mountains. As he always had lots of money with him, he found our inn the most secure place to stay.

Next morning, when servants had gone to serve his breakfast in his room, they found him dead in his bed. He was suffocated by pillow, and the murderer had stolen all his money. That incident made all the passengers frightened and all of them left the inn as soon as they got to know about it.

When the police came, there was no one except my family and servants and a dead body. My husband was old and soft-headed. After a long inspecting, the officers accused my poor husband of killing the merchant. They arrested him and took him with them. He was so kind-hearted. I wondered how he could be a murderer. When they were taking him, he was as silent as usual; perhaps he didn't know where they were taking him. He looked at Emily and me innocently who was just ten years old. It was the last time I saw him and after that I have never heard of him."

"What a strange destiny you have had!" exclaimed Edgar.

"Yes. After that disaster, nobody came to our inn. Gossips spread out everywhere that my husband was a murderer. After that, I lay off the servants and workers. Emily and I lived alone. I could never get over that disaster; the worse is that I still don't know where my poor husband is. I don't know if he is dead or alive." said the landlady. She put out her cigarette. Her daughter entered the kitchen. She sat beside her mother and started eating dinner.

"Excuse me, can I take a bath?" asked Edgar.

"Of course! It is upstairs at the end of the corridor. Do you want me to guide you?" said the landlady.

"No, thanks. I will find it myself." said Edgar and left the kitchen. Back to his room, Edgar took his towel and went to bathroom. It had a damaged door and it had too many gaps and notches that inside the bathroom could easily be seen. But there was a very thin and delicate curtain inside. He went in and undressed. While he was bathing, he noticed some sounds behind the door. He felt that someone is behind that gapped door. At first, he became uneasy, but then he thought that no one was there except Emily and her old mother. He became sure that he was in hallucination. He took a long bath and went to his room. He spent a comfortable night there after all things he had done all day long.

Next morning, he got up with a knock on the door. He put on his clothes right away and opened the door. It was Emily with a tray in her hands. He had brought breakfast for Edgar. She had decorated it with all they had in their kitchen.

"Good morning, sir. Here is your breakfast." said Emily.

"Good morning. Thank you." replied Edgar.

"I hope you enjoy it." replied Emily and made a sweet and enchanting smile on her beautiful lips. She put the tray on the table and stood up beside Edgar. She was wearing an open red dress that could be seductive for every young man. Her busty body was more attractive in her new dress. She continued her strange looks at Edgar and then left the room. Her cheeks had gone red.

Her behavior and kind of dressing was strange for handsome Edgar. It seemed she was trying to expose something, but it was not clear for Edgar whose mind was full of a girl he had seen the day before. He ate his breakfast and got ready to go to visit the old lady and her granddaughter. Downstairs, he saw the old landlady cleaning the room.

"Good morning, madam. Can I make a phone call?" requested Edgar.

"Hi. Of course, you can. There is a telephone on the corner." answered the landlady and pointed to the telephone. Even the telephone was dusty. It seemed that they hadn't used it for a long time; not even a single phone call. Edgar telephoned Mr. Robert and asked about the company. Then, he left the inn and decided to walk to the village instead of using his car.

He was walking carefully. He did not want anyone to see him. While Edgar was walking on the road side, a small lorry stopped before him. Behind the lorry was full of chopped trees and a young man was driving the lorry.

"Come up, man. I am going to the village." said the driver.

"Oh, thanks, I won't bother; I would walk." replied Edgar gently. Their gesticulations were familiar to each other. Then, Edgar looked again at the lorry and made a guess. This man could be his friend, Teddy, who worked as a carpenter at his father's shop. He got very happy and asked, "Sorry, may ask your name?"

"Teddy, my name is Teddy." answered the driver.

"Hey, Teddy. It's me, Edgar. Your old friend." replied Edgar happily. Teddy was completely surprised and he got out of the car at once. They hugged each other firmly. They were so happy. By seeing each other they remembered lots of sweet childhood memories.

They got on Teddy's small lorry and went toward the village. They spoke all that short distance and enjoyed their time. It was clear that the two old friends, seeing each other after years, could speak for days. But when they entered the village, Edgar got off the lorry and decided to walk the rest.

"But don't forget. Do not tell anyone about my being here; I would explain you latter." urged Edgar.

"No problem. I am always in the carpentry; you can come whenever you wish." replied Teddy and went off.

Edgar walked the alleys and reached the old lady's house. He rang the bell. The young, pretty girl opened the door. She was wearing a light olive dress which had made her much prettier. They both got happy seeing each other. Something had preoccupied Edgar, but he couldn't find the reason. Something appeared in front of his eyes and then disappeared immediately. It really had confused him.

The old lady was sitting on a rocker beside the window looking at the backyard. She was in white. The house was a very beautiful one and it was decorated elegantly; sure it was the girl's taste. He sat in front of the old lady and started speaking to her.

"What a cheerful morning it is!" said Edgar wearing a smile.

"Yes, my son. This view keeps me alive. Seeing the sun shining in the sky makes me calm and also the trees in the yard; most of them are my age." she said and moved her rocker.

"I am happy that you are in good health." said Edgar.

"Yes, I am very fine." she smiled and continued, "I want to know more about you young man, tell me about you."

Edgar then explained about himself and told the old lady about his work and life, but everything in present, and not his past. When he spoke about himself, the old woman was fully attentive to him. She enjoyed it when Edgar was speaking. She found Edgar wise and gentleman. But something was strange to her and it was why of Edgar's attention to them. She thought Edgar was in love with Flora. Flora was the name of the pretty girl. But it was just a guess; all due to Edgar's eyes on Flora.

After a while, young Flora brought Edgar and her grandmother some coffee. It was the most delicious coffee Edgar had ever drunk. Edgar was still looking at Flora and this made the virtuous girl look down in virtue. They were silent for a while, but the doorbell broke the silence. It was Mrs. Williams, the old friend of Flora's grandmother. Seeing Edgar in their home was very strange to her and she looked at him in a very different way. Maybe it could be a new topic for gossips in the village. Edgar was not comfortable in her presence and so, left there.

Once out of their house, he was careful not to be seen again. But he was totally preoccupied. He was thinking about Flora. Edgar's emotions toward her got stronger day in day out. He walked the whole path and went back to inn. He was very tired. He could think about nothing but Flora!

"Am I falling in love?" he thought to himself, "But no, it is not love; maybe it is. If it is not love, what could it be? Something attractive is making me closer to her. Her eyes and sights are different from everyone." asking such questions had baffled Edgar. He didn't go for lunch and rested on his bed the whole day.

About nine o'clock at night, he woke up by a horrible dream. When he woke up, he could not remember his terrible dream. He went to take a bath to get calm. Lights of the bathroom were on and he could hear the shower. He went closer. The door was closed, but as it was gabbed, he could see the inside easily. It was Emily. She was in birthday suit bathing in the bathroom. She didn't notice Edgar. But why was she bathing upstairs while their bathroom was downstairs beside their room? Looking at her busty wet body was enjoyable for every man, but Edgar turned back and went toward his room. He could hear a man speaking to the landlady downstairs. Hiding somewhere, Edgar looked at them. A tall man was speaking to the landlady. He was middle-aged and well-dressed. He was making his tie. He gave some money to the landlady and left the inn.

Edgar went back to his room. He felt that some strange things were going on in there. But he didn't notice and after eating dinner, without asking any questions, slept.

Next morning, he went to Flora and her grandmother. He did it every morning. Mrs. Williams, who had seen Edgar before in their home, saw him again; this made gossips spread faster in the village. It was said a gentleman and handsome young man visited Flora and her grandmother everyday. Also it was said that he was very rich and he was from city.

Those gossips spread so fast, and finally, Sara heard about that. Her friend, Julia, had heard about the gossips and told Sara about them. Julia was the closest friend of Sara and she knew that Sara had a deep emotion toward Edgar.

When Sara heard the news, she got shocked and sad at first, but then, she didn't believe it at all. She was sure that Edgar was not in the village and he had left there days ago. That man could not be the person who visited Flora. She told Julia that he could not be Edgar and it should be someone else.

Hearing the gossips, poor Edgar decreased his visits, and most of the time, stayed in the inn where strange things happened. Every night, a person came to the inn, but didn't stay there. He just stayed for a short while and then left the inn. Edgar could see him from the window of his room which was predominant to the yard. The strangest thing was that the man didn't go by the path and he always hid in the darkness of the woods. It had become a question for Edgar, but he didn't want to ask any questions from the landlady.

Days passed alike. One night, something strange happened to Edgar. He had gone to visit Flora and when he left there, he noticed a man staring at him while waving to Flora. Edgar looked at him, but he could not be recognized. His body was almost in the darkness. Edgar went closer to him, but he ran immediately and hid in the darkness. It was very queer to him. While he was walking in the dark alleys, he could again feel somebody following him, but he could see no one.

Next morning, Edgar left the inn and decided to go and visit his friend, Teddy. He found the carpentry with difficulty. He looked inside and saw Teddy's father beside him. His father had got older and didn't work as much. Teddy did all the stuff instead. Edgar stood outside on a corner waiting till Teddy's father left the carpentry. It took a bit long, but finally, he put on his clothes and left the carpentry.

Edgar went inside expecting a warmly welcome. But it wasn't like usual. Teddy almost cut him dead. He pretended not to have seen Edgar and went on working. Edgar got surprised. He thought that his friend could be sad.

"What is wrong with you, Ted?" asked Edgar and went closer to him. He stood beside Teddy.

"Nothing, nothing!" replied Teddy in a very small voice and got back to his job. The machine had made a loud sound in the shop. They could not hear each other properly. Edgar switched the machine off and put his hand on Teddy's shoulder, "I am sure you have got a problem. I have not ever seen you in such a sad condition. You can count on me."

"I said that nothing has happened. I'm just tired." answered Teddy and wore an artificial smile. Meanwhile, a young man entered the shop. He had black hair and round eyes.

"Hi, Teddy. How is it going, man?" asked the young man apparently in close relationship with Teddy.

"Hi, I am not good." answered Teddy contradicting what he told Edgar.

"Don't you want to introduce this guy? I do not think I have seen him before." said the young man and looked at Edgar. Edgar was behind Teddy still puzzled of why of Teddy's treating.

"Don't you know him? Look more; he is our old friend; you know him." answered Teddy and looked weirdly at Edgar. It seemed that he was not satisfied with him that day. He spoke acrimoniously to Edgar.

"What do you mean? I don't know this guy!" exclaimed the young man.

"He is Edgar; our old friend." said Teddy and then he forced a smile and continued, "You can never be a clever man, David."

Edgar again ran into one of his old friends. He was very happy to see him. Also, David got surprised seeing Edgar. They hugged each other warmly. David was the one who saved Edgar many years ago when he was about to drown in the river. He was frisky and happy as usual. Nothing could make him sad. David noticed Teddy was not in a good mood. He took Edgar's hand and they left the shop. Teddy again started working. He worked carelessly as he was not aware of what he was doing.

"Did you notice Teddy's strange behavior today?" asked Edgar curiously.

"It was not important." said David and smiled.

"But it was important to me; he had never greeted me in such a cold way. He spoke to me reluctantly. I am sure; there is a problem." answered Edgar seriously.

"Actually, he is sometimes the way you just saw. He loves a girl, but he can never express his love to her. He can never go closer to her. And sometimes, when he thinks more about her, he gets crazy and treats others so cold." answered David.

"Why cannot he express his love?" asked Edgar.

"This is my question, too. He thinks that the girl doesn't love him because she never looks at him when they face each other outside. I think she would look at him if she knows Ted loves her. It is not her fault because she doesn't know that somebody loves her." asserted David.

"I think we can help him. We can tell the girl about his love." said Edgar thinking so simple of Teddy's affair.

"No. It won't work. Once, I gave it a try, but Ted didn't let me. The worse is that he is worried about something else ..." said David left unsaid.

"What is that?" asked Edgar.

"He always thinks that someone else would rub his love before he can reach her." answered David. They talked about Teddy for a long time walking in the alleys. They tried to come up with a solution to help their friend. They were worried about their friend; loyal friend always think about each other.

"I never thought that love can be such a complex subject. I thought it was simple. I knew it as one short sight, as a glance. I always visualized the image of love in a happy gesture. But now, when I see Teddy, I have to have second thought about love. Now, I believe that love can be either the sign of happiness or sadness." said David.

"Love is something that we have to feel it with all our might in our heart and mind. Sometimes, these feelings become strange and we cannot recognize whether they are love or not."

"Love is something we can never define and perceive it" said David and laughed smoothly. They were still speaking about Teddy and love; at a turn of an alley, Edgar suddenly took David's hand and they ran to another narrow alley.

"What are you doing, man?" asked David.

"Did you see those two girls?" asked Edgar.

"Yes, they were Sara and her friend, Julia; why are you running from them?" asked David curiously.

"I am not. She must not see me here in the village. It has a long story; I would explain it to you later." answered Edgar hurriedly and they changed their path to other alleys. They went to the hill; to their childhood nest.

"Would you like to have a race like those times?" asked David.

"No, boy!" a lazy frown sat on Edgar's forehead, "I cannot run even for meters."

"Come on! You never ran even those times!" boasted David and laughed loudly. It was about noon when they reached the top of the hill. There were no clouds in the sky and the brilliant sun was shining with all her power. Looking at the village, Edgar could see all the houses from there. Seeing such a beautiful scene made him soulful. He again remembered all his childhood and his strange adventure.

"You didn't tell me about yourself, boy. What do you do? After your first latter, I never heard from you again." asked David and Edgar explained everything to him with all details. When he told him about the stone, David got completely shocked.

"How lucky you are! So, now you are a rich man. What are you doing here? Now, you should have a good life in the city, right?" asked David a bit enviously.

"Yes, I am a rich man and I have a lot of money; but money is not everything and sometimes even nothing. You see that today I am here in the village. It is not for money. Another emotional subject had attracted me here and it doesn't let me go.

Not all people there come from a comfortable background. Even the richest are immersed in daily problems. And after a short time, they work all day without any control. They waste most of their lives to earn money, and when they get rich, they are too old; they do their best to take care of their money." replied Edgar and sighed deeply.

"Aha, you wanted to tell about your being here. Why don't you want to be seen by others, especially Sara?" asked David curiously.

"I would tell you, but not now." Edgar said in a try to change the topic, "What do you do David?"

"You knew my father very well; he was always drunk and never worked. And my mother got sick and she couldn't work anymore. We had a field around the village. My brother and I started farming there. It has been a long time since we have been working there." David said and asked, "Can I ask you a question?"

"Of course!" replied Edgar.

"Do you know Julia? I mean Sara's best friend?" asked David.

"Not really, I have just heard her name from Sara! Do you love her?" asked Edgar making a rapid guess about David.

"I'm charmed by her. I really do. But I never find any good situation to express my love to her. Once I saw her and we spoke together, but exactly when I wanted to speak about my love, Sara came and they went." David said.

"Wow! All my friends are in love." exclaimed Edgar and smiled.

"I'm sure you are in love, too." answered David at once.

"I am not. In fact, there is a person in my life that attracts me, but I cannot see it as a love." replied Edgar. They spoke for a long time about love and being in love. After a while Edgar, left David and walked toward the inn.

Edgar was weary of the long walk when he reached the inn. Emily and her mother were eating lunch in the kitchen. When Edgar entered the kitchen, Emily stood up immediately and prepared some food for Edgar. She stared at him while Edgar was eating.

After lunch, Edgar went to his room and slept all the evening. He was very tired. At about midnight, he woke up hearing loud noises. The landlady was arguing with a man. Edgar went to the stairs and saw the same man. But this time they were arguing loudly.

Edgar decided to go to them and get to know the stranger, but he again changed his mind and stayed in the stairs, until the stranger gave some money to the landlady and left hastily.

"Who is he? What is he doing here every night? The landlady said they had no relatives. It is very strange. He pays the landlady every night. But, what for?" thought Edgar. He was confused about the events in the inn. When he went back to his room, he heard the sound of water from the bathroom again. Someone was bathing there. Edgar went closer and looked inside and again he saw Emily bathing there. Her bare and wet body shone under the shower. Edgar turned around immediately and went to his room. When he closed the door, Emily came out of the bathroom and ran downstairs.

"What is going on here?" thought Edgar. Then, he went to bed and slept. Soon, it started to rain. Raindrops kissed the window. It rained all night long.

Next morning, the entire garden was wet and a shiny sun ruled the sky of the village. Edgar woke up late at about ten o'clock—not in the habit of getting up early any longer. He put away the curtain and looked outside and saw the beautiful morning. On the other side of the road, he saw Teddy in his lorry. Edgar called him out loud, but Teddy didn't hear him and whizzed off.

When he came back to make his bed, Edgar faced a very strange scene. There was a big red spot on the right corner of his pillow; in a special shape like two lips. He got shocked seeing it. He was alone all the night and his door was locked. No one could enter his room. Most importantly, there wasn't anyone in the inn to enter his room. But the red spot was there as if someone had kissed the pillow.

Edgar left the inn and went outside for a walk. He was surprised about the events in the inn. He was walking through the woods not knowing where he was going. After a while, he found himself in the entrance of the village. He went under the bridge and sat beside the river. A man caught him from back. Edgar was afraid. He turned back and saw his friend. It was Bob with a bag in his hand. He was in brown.

"I thought you had gone." said Bob.

"Yes, but I had to come back." answered Edgar.

"What are you doing here, man?" asked Bob and sat beside Edgar on the grass. Bob put his bag on a stone.

"I really don't know." replied Edgar shrugging his shoulders off.

"What do you mean? I have never seen you like this! What is wrong with you?" asked Bob again.

"I am in a very big dilemma. Now, I should have been in the city doing my job, but I am here. I cannot leave this village." replied Edgar.

"What is this attractive thing which keeps you here?" asked Bob.

"I love someone, but I don't think it is love. She is very attractive for me, she is very important. Even I can't leave her and go to city. But something in my heart tells me that it is not love. So, what can it be?

I am doubtful." said Edgar opening his heart for a friend for the first time.

"Wow! Who is this lucky girl you love?"

"Her name is Flora. She is very beautiful, very kind; and she beyond one's imagination." said Edgar throwing stones in the river.

"Flora? I don't know her. In fact, I don't know the young girls of the village. But I know the kids well, because I teach them at school." Bob said and then looked at his watch, "Oh! It is late; I have to go to school. We will talk it over later." Then he left Edgar and went toward school. Edgar kept alone for hours beside the river. Throwing stones into the water, Edgar thought about Flora.

At about noon, he left there and went to see Flora. On the path, he again saw Sara and Julia. They were buying bread. He tried to hide, but Sara saw him from back. She left her friend and followed him. On a corner, Edgar ran and she couldn't find him. Sara went back to Julia doubtful whether or not to have seen Edgar.

"Were did you go?" asked Julia.

"I think I saw Edgar. I didn't see his face. But he looked like him. He was handsome and nice. I followed him, but he disappeared."

"You have been hallucinated. You yourself said he had left the village a few days ago. What for should he come back?" said Julia and made a mocking laugh.

"I have really missed him. When he was far away for years I missed him less. But now, when I saw him some days ago, I miss him more." said Sara and sighed.

Edgar got calm to have missed the danger. He walked off fast and reached Flora's home immediately. She was in the garden watering the plants. She didn't notice Edgar. She was singing very slowly; it was not clearly heard.

Edgar went closer to her and picked a flower from the garden.

“Hi, Flora. Good afternoon.” greeted Edgar. Flora got shocked and turned around. She saw Edgar in front of her eyes. The water hose fell down from her hands.

“Hi ….” the virtuous girl said, “You … surprised me.”

“Excuse me; I didn’t mean it.” said Edgar and gave her the flower. She took the flower proving her goodness. Then, she offered Edgar to go inside.

“No, thanks. I think we can walk for a short time in the garden. Do you agree?” said Edgar persuasively.

“No problem.” accepted Flora and hoisted her head. Her eyes were very beautiful and charming. No logic could deny those charming eyes.

They had a big garden behind the building. Tall trees around the garden had made a big and cool shadow. There was an old, wooden bench beside a small pond. They sat there and spoke. All the red fish in the water could hear their words.

“Where is your grandmother?” asked Edgar.

“She was a bit sick today. She coughed a lot. I gave her drugs. She slept.” replied Flora.

“Why do you live alone with your grandmother? Where are your parents?” asked Edgar.

“They left me when I was kid. My grandmother says that they had to go from here, but she never tells me why.”

“Do you miss them?”

“How can I miss one I have never seen? My grandmother had never lets me miss anything. She is very kind. But I believe that I will see my parents one day.” answered Flora.

As they spoke, they felt closer. Passing time, Flora felt less shy and could speak to Edgar more comfortably. She was very glad that Edgar had given her a flower and she was playing with that all the time.

“There is something I want to tell you, but I didn’t have the time to say it before.” said Edgar precipitately.

"What is that? Say it now, I listen." said Flora and smiled sweetly; she could possibly guess what to hear.

"In fact, I myself don't know what it is exactly; I cannot put it into the words." answered Edgar in gasps. He could hardly ever put his emotions across. He couldn't unscramble terms to his feelings. Now, he wanted to express his strongest emotions. He kept playing with his fingers or the bench.

"Sorry, I don't get you." said Flora surprised. At that time, she heard her grandmother calling her.

"Oh! It is grandmother. She is calling me. Let's go inside." said Flora.

"Of course." agreed Edgar. Perhaps, he had to thank grandmother for saving him. If she didn't call Flora, Edgar didn't know what to tell her. Again, he had to keep his emotions in his heart until some other time.

When they entered home, grandmother got very happy to see Edgar. She loved him a lot and she always got happy when he saw Flora beside him. She believed Edgar is whom Flora can trust. She never let Flora to speak to other men.

Edgar stayed there all day. After lunch, he again spoke with Flora for a long time. Now, they were completely close friends. Flora didn't feel shy anymore. After dinner, Edgar decided to go. When he left the home, Flora accompanied him in the garden. They walked to the gate.

"Today was a great day for me." said Edgar and smiled.

"Same here. I could speak to someone. Speaking with you was a great glory."

"Tomorrow, I will come to you again."

"I'll be seeing you." said Flora and made a beautiful smile on her red lips.

Edgar bent, took Flora's hand, and kissed her smooth hands in that moonlit night. It was a great scene for both of them; chiefly Edgar, but a sudden voice broke their beautiful silence. Someone broke a glass in the alley. Edgar turned around and again saw someone on the corner looking at them. He immediately left Flora and went toward that man in the darkness. When Edgar went closer to him, the man ran away and Edgar followed him this time.

Nothing was clear in the darkness. Just two men were running after each other in the alleys. Flora got very disturbed, but she immediately went back to home pretending to look after her grandmother.

Edgar was still following the stranger. He was running so fast and Edgar couldn't catch him. They ran so long a distance; out of the village, they went to the woods. Everywhere was silent and nothing but the two running after each other. Suddenly, the stranger hid in the woods. Edgar could see no one in the utter darkness.

Edgar got disappointed to find the man and decided to come back.

"Why should I follow that man?" thought Edgar. But then he answered, "If there was not anything wrong, why he ran when I tried to get closer?" Asking this question from himself, Edgar looked around himself again. But when he didn't see anything in the darkness, he decided to go back. He had a long way to go back to the inn.

At the moment of the first step, he heard a noise. Someone was groaning in the woods. He followed the noise. Someone was drowning in the swamp. He couldn't see his face, but he was the stranger.

Edgar immediately found a big piece of wood and stretched it toward the drowning man. He took the wood and got out of the swamp. His face was muddy; it had blackened by sludge. The stranger again tried to run, but Edgar took his hand and put him down on the grass. Then he cleaned the stranger's mien with his sleeve. He didn't let Edgar do it, but Edgar did it and finally saw his face. Edgar couldn't believe what he was seeing. He was completely shocked. It was Teddy. The man, whom he followed, was his close friend. But what was the reason? Why Teddy was escaping from Edgar.

"Why are you escaping from me?" asked Edgar ready to know why.

"Leave me alone, Edgar. Please, leave me alone." shouted Teddy reluctant to look at Edgar. Maybe Teddy didn't dare to.

"I would never leave you here in this condition. I don't understand why you are treating me like this. Yesterday, I came to your carpentry, but you didn't greet me like you used to and I noticed your strange behavior. But I didn't tell you. And today, you were keeping an eye on me; you escaped when I tried to get closer. What does all this mean, Ted?" asked Edgar angrily.

"I prefer to keep silent. Actually, I have nothing to say; leave me alone …" shouted Teddy.

"You have … you must tell me about your preoccupation. If I am a guilty, then I should know my sin." replied Edgar emphatic on every word. Just then, Teddy stood up and shouted staring at Edgar's eyes, "You are a robber; a traitor …" He turned and walked off. His words were shocking to Edgar. He didn't understand why he should be a robber, why he should be traitor. He again followed Teddy and stopped him.

"Why do you think I am a robber? What did I rob from you?" asked Edgar.

"You are a love robber. You have robbed your friend's love. You, traitor!" answered Teddy and burst into tears.

"What do you mean? Who is your love? Who have I robbed?" asked Edgar deeply bewildered.

"Flora …!" said Teddy and ran away.

"But wait … wait, Ted. You are wrong." shouted Edgar. But Teddy didn't listen and went off. Now, Edgar was alone in the utter darkness again in new mire. Only stars could see him in that chaos. His heart was thumping harder under that pressure. His feet became weak. He walked wearily.

He walked through the woods and reached the inn. All the lights of the inn were off except the kitchen. Edgar entered the kitchen and saw Emily sitting on a chair. Edgar was wet and all muddy. Emily got shocked seeing him in that condition.

"What has happened to you, sir?" she asked.

"Nothing … I slipped in sludge. Why haven't you slept yet? It's very late." said Edgar.

"I was waiting for you; you would never come late. I got worried." she said and made a cup of coffee for Edgar. They sat around the table in front of each other. A cup of coffee was what Edgar needed.

"You look very disturbed tonight; I have never seen you like this." asked Emily and stared at his eyes.

"It is all about love; a devious that leads everyone to nowhere." replied Edgar in a very small voice sipping his coffee.

"Are you in love with someone?" asked Emily curiously.

"Maybe, but I don't know for sure. The amazing thing is that today love put me in a dilemma. I am being a victim of this devious. Today, my best friend thought a traitor of me. He called me a robber; robber of love. How can I be a traitor to a friend whom I love?" said Edgar. When Emily heard this, a mask of curiosity covered her visage. She asked, and Edgar explained the whole story to her. He explained all his emotions about Flora to her.

"So, you are not guilty; you didn't know that your friend loved her." uttered Emily.

"I know, but Teddy doesn't. I see him. He is immersed in love and love is blind. But I can't tolerate his attitude toward me as a traitor or robber. Ted is my friend and I don't like to offend him." said Edgar.

"You should have explained everything to him." suggested Emily, but a bit late.

"He didn't let me. He just said Flora's name and left soon. I can feel that he hates me. He believes me as his foe, not his friend. He even didn't like to look at me." answered Edgar. He spoke to Emily until late and then went to his room. Edgar put his head on the pillow, but couldn't sleep. He was just thinking about the events of that night; once to Flora and then to Teddy. It was the biggest dilemma he had ever had.

The following day, he stayed in bed until late. Emily woke him up by knocking on the door. Edgar was weary and reluctantly opened his eyes.

He had slept very late the night before. After a small meal, he decided to see David. Maybe he could help Edgar. He was a friend of both. He could probably solve the problem; to help Edgar out of that whirlpool.

He found David working on his field. He was alone and his brother was not there. When he heard that Edgar was calling him, he came toward him.

"Hi, good morning. What are you doing here?" asked David and put his spade aside.

"Hi." Edgar said sadly, "I have to speak to you. I'm not in a good situation."

"It's clear! You aren't bright. Surly, you have a big problem. You aren't the same Edgar." claimed David.

"Yes, last night I figured out why Teddy was acting so strange that day."

"I told you the reason." David went on curiously, "Is there anything else?"

Edgar explained him the whole story. He expressed all the incidents that had happened to him the previous night. It was not a credible story for David.

'So, you both love one girl!" asked David to make sure.

"You can say that; Teddy did not take the right way. He treated me as a foe." answered Edgar.

"I know what you say. But you should understand him. He has loved that girl for a long time. And worst of all, he could never express his love to her. Meanwhile, you have been igniting the fire of jealousy in his heart; keeping seeing Flora I mean. Lovers are blind people, Ed. They aren't those they used to be. They feel everything thru emotions." said David.

"Maybe he is right. But I didn't know about his love. Once, he saw me exiting their house, but the next day, instead of telling the story to me, he just acted me like strangers." said Edgar in a small voice. He sat down beside the narrow stream and put his hand in the cold water.

"I said; he is a lover. He does not take in things now; fully out of wisdom! You are back after a long time and don't know Flora for so long. You could be worse than Teddy not in a far day. If you have a flame of love, Teddy has a hell of that. He is burning a thousand times more." answered David.

"But I'm sure we are of the same feelings. When I think about Flora, I feel so strange. Nothing else seems more important to me. She differs from everyone. But I don't know the reason."

"The reason?" David asked surprisingly, "Is there any reason but love. You love that girl; so does Teddy. But the difference is that, you don't want to believe it."

"What can I do? Do you have any idea to take me out of this dilemma?" begged Edgar.

"What can I say? I cannot tell any of you to stop your love. It is not to stop it even if we want. It grows by itself. No one can stop it." answered David with his wide-open hands depicting the impossibility.

"I know; I have to leave here. She belongs to Teddy. He loved her before me. I came late, and now, I have to go soon. I have no right on Flora." said Edgar sadly.

"Do you think it is the last way?" asked David.

"Yes. I wish I had never seen Flora. She gave a new meaning to my life. But now I have to be the previous Edgar. I have to go back to city, work in the company, and pass my usual life. Perhaps I won't disturb Teddy anymore." said Edgar tears rolling in his eyes; another cry destined in his life. But this time, everything was different. Only the shiny drops could heal his pain. Then, he continued in a very small voice, "But help them reach each other. Sure they will make a good couple. Tell Teddy I never wanted to disturb him." Saying these words, he stood up and left David. His footsteps were short. He went into the woods without knowing where he was going.

Meanwhile, another bad accident happened to poor Edgar. While walking, he entered the garden in which Mr. White's house stood. He didn't notice around himself, but others did.

A girl called him from behind, but Edgar again didn't notice. But when the girl appeared in front of his eyes, Edgar understood where he was. It was Sara who was shocked seeing Edgar; not only by seeing Edgar, but also by seeing him in that strange confusion. She was very angry with him. She could never believe that Edgar would hide anything from her anytime. She walked away angrily without saying a word. She felt so sad deep inside. Leaving him, Edgar regained his consciousness and forgot about his own problem and followed Sara.

She was sitting in a shadow of an old tree. She was crying under her lips and was playing with a small yellow flower in is beautiful hands. Edgar sat beside her, but he didn't know what to say. Again words failed him to express his feelings. He couldn't see Sara crying. She didn't look at him and it made him more uneasy. Maybe in that time the small flower in her hands was more important to her than poor Edgar.

"Do not cry, please. I can explain it. Please …" begged Edgar.

"What do you have to say? I know everything because I have heard things about a gentleman. These days everyone is speaking about you. But I never decided to believe them. I thought that if you came to village again, I would be the first one to know. How does it feel? I denied all the gossips, but supposedly I have to believe them." replied Sara murmuring.

"But you don't why I am here; you should listen to me."

"I know why you are here. Gossips are not always false. And I know who you have been meeting all this time." said Sara this and made a sardonic smile.

"How beautifully the news is spreading along the village. But you can't realize why I had to come back here."

"I can; I heard that in that house there is a girl called Flora. I heard that she is very pretty and charming. I heard that you love her and she is the only reason of your being here." shouted Sara and stood up to go.

"But this is not right, strange things have happened to me. I myself am confused. She had just taken my attention in an accident. That's all. I was trying to know the reason of this attraction, and today, I was about to leave here; believe me." said Edgar.

"You are deceiving yourself. Nothing could be the reason of a gentleman attracted to a young girl but love."

"You will be seeing me leave here today." claimed Edgar.

"Don't worry; you don't have to lie anymore. I won't tell anyone that I saw you. I never wanted to disturb you; neither do I now; because I always … I always …" Sara was left unsaid.

"Because what?" asked Edgar surprisingly.

"Forget it; I wish you a life full of prosperity." Hoped Sara, burst into the tears, and left Edgar. The misfortunes of the poor gentleman increased day after day.

He walked toward inn and decided to leave the village immediately and forget all the events that had happened in that short time.

"I have to leave here with all the memories. I have to forget beautiful looks of Flora. She belongs to Teddy because he is sure of his Love. I bothered everyone; Teddy, Sara, others. I should never come back." thought Edgar.

Sara, on the other side, had gone to her friend Julia. She needed someone to sympathize with her and the only one was her friend Julia.

"You are bothering yourself. He never belonged to you; never would he. You have to forget him." said Julia.

"I thought that I am the closest person in his life. He always wrote me letters whereas he did for no one else. He never forgot me. But now she loves a girl." said Sara crying in Julia's bosom.

"He is free to love anyone he wants. You cannot force him to love you. You are still his best friend, but you are not his love. Try to believe it. Writing a letter to a close friend is not the reason of loving her." said Julia and caressed her friend. Suddenly, someone hit the window of her room with a small stone.

"What was it?" asked Sara worriedly.

"Don't worry; I don't know who he is! But everyday, he throws a stone at my window to take me beside the window. Once, I could see him, but I didn't recognize him. I have learnt his trick and don't go beside the window anymore." said Julia and laughed.

"Maybe he is expressing his love in this way." said Sara and they laughed together. But very soon, Sara got sad again when she remembered Edgar.

Edgar reached and entered the inn so disturbed. His eyebrows were broken; his hair was tousled; he looked anxious. His weak steps tiredly took him upstairs. He staggered to his room and packed his assets and went downstairs.

"Are you leaving?" said someone from behind. It was Emily who had leaned to the wall crossing her hands at her chest.

"Yes. Everything is over for me here. There is no reason to stay longer. I came here and bothered some people. I told you once, love is a devious. It took me here for a while, and now, it is throwing me away from here. We are all under its control; love of everything; love of a person or love of a thing. It doesn't differ. Some people love money and so love guides them everywhere needed and they do everything to reach their love. Love is love. But matters of love are different. Different loves for different people." said Edgar slowly and took other steps to exit the inn.

"Do you think leaving is the last and best way?" asked Emily.

"Yes, sometimes we should struggle in the battle, but sometimes the best way is to wince and leave the battle; because when we leave that battle, it would change to peace. Love is the biggest battle of the world." replied Edgar.

"But I think you have to think more. Stay for tonight and think more. Tomorrow morning, if you were still determined to go, then leave here." urged Emily.

"No, sooner or later I have to go, so it is better to leave right away. I am habited to lose my dears. When I was a young boy, I lost all my family. Now, I am older and I can get along with this situation better." said Edgar and left the inn. When he was about to exit the yard, he saw a girl running toward him. She was very disturbed and in hurry. Edgar got shocked when the girl came closer and he saw her face. She was Flora. She had run all the way. Tired and out of breath, Flora couldn't speak a word. She was just breathing in pants. Edgar was still shocked seeing Flora there. Flora rested for a short while and then started to speak.

"You ... you have to come with me; grandmother ... grandmother ..."

"What? Grandmother what?"

"She is very sick ...! She is worse than ever before." said Flora with an overflow of sadness in her face.

"Why don't you call the doctor?" asked Edgar suggestively.

"She doesn't let me do that. She just asked me to take you to her." said Flora surprised at what she was asked for.

"How did you find me here?" Edgar asked surprisingly.

"It was not too hard. These days, everybody speaks about a stranger gentleman who stays in this strange, deserted inn. I could easily guess that you were that person." said Flora.

"Okay!" Edgar said hurriedly, "Let's go." They left the inn. Emily was looking at them thru the window. She could see that how much important Flora was to him. A small envy was drawn in her eyes. Edgar and Flora were running in the drive of the inn toward the road. Edgar forgot his own car which was parked in the yard as he was in hurry. They stood in the roadside in order to catch someone to drive them to village. Flora was as much tired as she could not even walk for a meter. After a short while they saw a small lorry coming toward them. It was going to village. There were some pieces of wood behind it.

Edgar got happy to see the lorry. It could drive them to village soon. But when the lorry came closer everything changed. His eyes got bigger. He got completely shocked when he saw Teddy.

Teddy was shocked and also angry to see Edgar and Flora in the roadside. He was definitely forming bad thoughts. Hi judged it the worst. He was angry enough to even kill his friend who was a foe now. But when he looked at Flora, he could not think about anything except her. He stopped down the road.

Edgar was reluctant to get on his lorry because he knew what was on his friend's mind; but when he remembered grandmother, he tried to hurry. Then they got on the lorry and went toward the village.

Teddy was completely silent. Once, thinking about Edgar, he got angry, but about Flora, Teddy got calmer. He could see her in the right outside mirror of the lorry. He was confused that why she was so much disturbed.

When they arrived home, Edgar asked Teddy to come in; maybe he could help him. They entered home and immediately went to Grandmother's room. Teddy knew whose home it was. It was Mrs. Bell's home. She was in the bed. Teddy stood on a corner and shook his head. He was ashamed. He would never imagine being in Flora's home. Edgar and Flora went to Mrs. Bell's bed and sat around it. She was coughing terribly. Then, she turned her face to Edgar and looked at him for a while without a word.

"Grandmother? Let's take you to a doctor." requested Edgar.

"No, my son. I don't need a doctor." Then, she turned to Flora and said, "Would you please leave us alone? I want to speak to Edgar in confidence." Saying this Flora and Teddy left the room and closed the door. Teddy was completely ashamed. He could never imagine to seat side by side with Flora. But he never wished to see his love in that disturbed situation. She was like seared flowers. She was very worried about her grandmother. Flora had no one except her in her life. Teddy couldn't see Flora cry. He took out a piece of tissue and gave it to her to clean her tears. Teddy couldn't see the tears falling down on her cheeks. Her cheeks had gone pale. Her lips where trembling slowly when she cried.

"Thank you, sir." said Flora and took the tissue. Teddy's hand was shaking when he gave the tissue to her.

"You're welcome." answered Teddy in a very small voice.

"Are you a friend of Mr. Oliver?" asked Flora. Her question disturbed Teddy. He believed Edgar as his foe, but he could not tell Flora the story. How could he call his friend as his foe?

"Yes, we are friends."

In the other room, Edgar and grandmother were speaking to each other. Grandmother was speaking slowly. She was breathing with difficulty. Her heartbeats were slow. Her face was pale. But still she had her beautiful smile on her lips.

"Why don't you let us call a doctor?" asked Edgar again.

"There is no need. Sometimes, when people are dying they feel the smell of death, and now, I can feel this smell with all my heart. It's surrounded in the room. But you can't smell it." said the old lady serenely.

"No … no … don't tell these words. You would get better." answered Edgar while some small drops where rolling in the corner of his eyes. He loved grandmother as his own.

"Look over there. There is a chest of drawers; open the third one. There is a paper in there. Bring it here." said grandmother. Edgar stood up and brought the paper. It was written by grandmother.

"This is my will in which I leave all my assets to you. And the best and most important is Flora. I believe after my death the only one who can take care of Flora is you. You are the one on whom she can rely. Flora never trusted anyone and she didn't have any friends. But I saw that she had kind attitudes toward you. I don't tend to reveal the secret of this faith; now read the will." murmured grandmother and looked at Edgar. Edgar was still in shocked silence. Right at the moment of leaving a battle, he had to enter another; and this time, harder than before. He opened the paper and he just looked at the words without paying attention to the meaning of them, as he just wanted to obey the old lady's order. But the signature of the letter took all his attention. It had been written, "Anna Bell.". Her last name was familiar to him. Mrs. Bell. He become silent and thought about her last name.

"What are you thinking about?" remarked Mrs. Bell.

"Your last name is very familiar to me. I think I have heard it before, but I can't remember where." said Edgar.

"Names seem familiar to our ears a lot. I have never asked your name. I always called you my son. And even your name in the letter is blank. What is your name?" asked Mrs. Bell.

"Edgar Oliver"

"You have a beautiful name. Write your full name in the blank. Years ago, there was a small Edgar in the village. He worked in Mr. White's supermarket. He was very polite and active; exactly like you. After some time, he didn't work in the supermarket and I never asked Mr. White about him. I heard that poor Mr. White is sick, too. He is a very good man. I hope he gets better soon." Mrs. Bell said. When he said those sentences, Edgar started to cry from depth of his heart. He took Mrs. Bell's hand and kissed it.

"Why are you crying, Edgar?" asked grandmother with her beautiful smile still on her lips.

"I am the same Edgar. I am the shop-boy of Mr. White." said Edgar in a small voice and cleaned his tears. Grandmother's eyes burst into tears, too. Even crying was hard for him in that situation.

"And now, I remember you. Once, I took your stuff to your home and you gave me three dollars as bonus. And those three dollars made me so rich. I always owe you." said Edgar.

"You never owe me. I remember that day. When I gave you the money, you said in beautiful voice that you hoped you could requite my kindness one day. And you did it when you took me to hospital weeks ago. Now, I can trust you more than ever. I want to tell you a secret." said Mrs. Bell more slowly.

"What is that?" asked Edgar.

"It is about Flora. She is not my own grandchild. She was a small girl with beautiful hair. I saw from the window. She was crying in the yard. She was very frightened. I went out immediately and looked around. There was no one around her. She was alone. I figured out that she was lost. I hugged her and caressed her. She became calmer. I took her in and gave her some food. She was hungry. She was eating rapidly and I was looking at her beauty. She was like a doll. After eating food, I took her out to find her parents. No one knew her. At night, we came back home. I never had a daughter. I was alone, too. I decided to keep her with me till I would find her parents. But I never could find any address of them. The only sign of the little girl was a necklace on his neck. She still has it." said Mrs. Bell. Her fingers in Edgar's hand become weak and they fell down. She closed her eyes and never opened again. She slept forever. Edgar shouted to call Flora and Teddy.

Chapter 8

There weren't many people around the grave. Nobody knew the silent death of Mrs. Bell. When the undertaker poured the last shovel of soil on the coffin, every one left the place but Edgar, Flora, and Teddy. Flora could not leave her grandmother; a grandmother who was not a real one. She felt herself the loneliest in the world. She felt no one around herself. But her destiny would not tell this.

Edgar kept looking at Flora. He believed that he had found the secret of his attraction to her. He remembered Mrs. Bell's last words. The old lady had opened a new page in Edgar's book of life.

They left the graveyard and went home. At the moment of their arrival, Flora burst into tears again. She had missed her grandmother. That big house without kind Mrs. Bell was like a deserted home. All the plants in the garden were sear and faint. They all had missed the kind grandmother of the house.

Edgar still was looking at Flora. He was murmuring something under his lips instinctively. It was something like saying Lisa. He was calling Lisa from his heart. He took out his necklace and showed it to Flora. She got shocked. She had the same.

"They are same, aren't they?" exclaimed Edgar quietly.

"Yes … it is very strange …" said Flora with owe.

"Yes, it *is* strange; and it would be stranger when I say there is a mother mark on your left shoulder. I am sure about it." said Edgar. Flora got shocked again. She left Edgar and went to a corner. She got angry with him. She was confused that how he knew about her mother mark on her left shoulder. For a while, she suspected him. But she could never imagine Edgar as wicked. Teddy was shocked by Edgar's utterances. Disgust was drawn in his eyes. Again the sinister thoughts came to his mind. He couldn't stop himself and he decided to leave.

"No, Teddy. Stop! You should be here." said Edgar and then tuned to Flora and repeated his question.

"How do you know that there is a mother mark on my left shoulder?" asked Flora nervously. Teddy went beside the window and looked out at the garden.

"I know it because I hugged you when you were born. I know it because I can never forget that night. I know it, because you are not Flora;" Edgar hesitated, "and you never were … you are Lisa. You are always Lisa. I am your brother. I am Edgar who lost you many years ago and today destiny again brought us face to face." said Edgar and cleaned the drops falling down from his eyes.

Flora and also Teddy were shocked by the words they heard from Edgar. She was to faint that Edgar caught her in his hands. Lisa was in her brother's bosom. She could feel reliance in his hands. Everything was clear for Lisa to believe her brother, signs, emotions, and their sight. Tears in her eyes dried and changed to a sweet smile on her lips.

In the other side of the room, Teddy was happy. Edgar's words were the best news for him. But he was ashamed. He had judged erroneously about Edgar. He never believed his friend. He was in a strange uncomfortable situation. Teddy left there and went out.

"I could never forgive myself after losing you. If I hadn't closed my eyes that day, I would have had you in front of my eyes all these long years." stated Edgar with a burden of regret of losing all those years.

"There is nothing to be forgiven; you didn't do that on purpose; it was an accident. It was our destiny." answered Lisa and simply laughed.

"I looked for you days and nights. I could never find a sign of you. Days were passing one after the other, but I couldn't find you. I have a lot to tell ..." Edgar took a breath, "I had a very strange life all these years."

"Where are our parents, Edgar?" asked Lisa in a sad voice.

"We lost them in a volcano eruption. You were too little to recognize the situation. You slept soon on my knees. Our father was a hero. He sacrificed himself to save our mother, but they were both surrounded with magma and I didn't see anything anymore. I could just hear the voice of their love even from miles away." said Edgar.

"How did our mother look like?" asked Lisa.

"She was beautiful like you. She was kind and good; an earthly angel. That night was very cold and you were coughing. When we were running toward the river to get in the boats, she suddenly turned back to bring your blanket. But when he exited from home he faced the melted material in front of her feet." said Edgar and some small tears rolled in the corner of his eyes.

"I could never have an imagination of my parents. Sometimes, I dreamed a horrible scene. I dreamed that a woman in the fire was asking me to help her, but very soon the fire changed to a beautiful field." said Lisa.

"During these long years, I never went back to our own land. I never dared to see our burned house. I never wanted to remember those terrible memories. " uttered Edgar.

"But I love to see where I was born. I love to see my own village." said Lisa imploringly.

"If you desire, we will go; now I think myself as the happiest person in the world beside you. I can't believe that you are in front of my eyes." said Edgar. He and Lisa spoke for a long time that day. They wanted to speak more than years that they were far away from each other. They had a lot to speak about and tell each other.

Next day early in the morning, Edgar went to Teddy. He was not in the carpentry. He found him alone in a garden. He was immersed in thinking under the shadow of a tree. Teddy got shocked and kept his head down in shyness.

"Why are you still acting strangely? I thought that everything was solved between us." said Edgar and looked at Teddy, but he didn't say any words and kept silent staring at the grass. "Look … you shouldn't keep silent; you need to tell me everything. We are still close friends." said Edgar.

"I was wrong about you." said Teddy in a small voice.

"What do you mean?" asked Edgar.

"I judged faultily about you. I was not a good friend for you! I accused you because you loved your own sister." tried Teddy to put his thoughts into words.

"You don't need to speak so. I have forgotten all recent happenings. Now, when I have found Lisa, I can't think about anything else." said Edgar and gave Teddy a feeling of comfort. When they came back to village, Edgar decided to visit Mr. White and his family, and also Mr. Tomas; but he decided to go there by Lisa. In the path, he spoke about Mr. White and his family. Lisa, thus, got eager to see them.

Ringing the doorbell, Edgar and Lisa waited behind the door. It was Mary who opened the door. Seeing Edgar made her happy, but she was astounded to see a girl beside him. She had never seen Lisa before. Meanwhile, Sara was coming down from the stairs with a tray in her hands. Sparkle of jealousy ignited in her heart. She didn't know what to say except a very small hello. She went to her mother and stood beside her. She was squeezing her dress.

Edgar went upstairs to visit Mr. White, and so did Lisa. Mr. White had grown weaker and weaker. He could greet Edgar hard.

"Hi, dear Mr. White. How are you?"

"Hi, my son; not so good. I'm not the strong man you knew. Who is this pretty girl beside you?" said Mr. White and smiled looking at Lisa.

How alone he was on the bed in a corner of the room! He could not even move his hands properly.

"She is all my life." said Edgar this and someone behind the door made a strange sound. It was Sara who heard Edgar's word. She was to cry. She didn't want to believe that someone else is Edgar's life and love. More strange, she didn't understand why Edgar had taken the girl beside himself to their home. Sara couldn't stop anymore behind the door. She left there for her room and cried there.

"She is whom I always waited for. She is whom I always missed. Maybe you don't believe when I say her name. She is Lisa, my sister, who I lost years ago and now I found her after these long years." said Edgar and looked at Lisa. Mary, on her way to room, got shocked by hearing that, and so did Mr. White. They both looked at Lisa. They only could speak by their sights. Most of the times, words are too low to express emotions.

"Where is Sara; she will be happy if she hears it." Edgar asked Mary.

"She must be here. She came upstairs before me." answered Mary still starring at Lisa.

"I know where I can find her." asserted Edgar and left the room. He directly went to Sara's room. When Edgar opened the door, Sara was looking outside the window. When Edgar went closer, he saw some tears on Sara's beautiful cheeks. She had cried. When Edgar wanted to speak, Sara cut in on his speech, "You don't need say anything. I heard everything." And again, she burst into tears and turned her face away.

"But you are wrong; as usual. You never wanted to hear all my words."

"What do you want to say? Do you want to repeat that she is all your life?"

"I still say that she is all my life because she is my sister; she is Lisa. She is the one I always waited for all my life." stated Edgar and gave Sara a big shock. Sara was about to fall down that Edgar took her and hugged her in his bosom. She was pell-mell. She was breathing hastily. She was pale in face. She couldn't look at Edgar's eyes.

In this moment, while Sara was in Edgar's bosom, Lisa and Mary entered the room. They both laughed seeing that scene. And it made Edgar and Sara laugh as well.

That day, they all spent the whole day together and about night Mr. Tomas joined them. He visited his old friend every night. His wearing style had changed to a countryman. He was more cheerful since Edgar last saw him and when he knew the news of Lisa and Edgar he became happier. They all passed a happy night and decided to go to Edgar and Lisa's village all together the next day.

That night, some eyes were not shot. Sara was immersed in thinking about Edgar. She could feel no rival in her love to him anymore. She felt the stars of the sky were more beautiful than ever before. Lisa was thinking about the next day. She was very eager to see her birthplace. Edgar was worried. He never dared to go back to his village, where he had bad memories. He knew that if he went there, he would remember that terrible rainy night. He knew that he would remember the colors of that night.

Next early morning, everyone was ready to set off. Mr. White was surrounded in a brown blanket and he could laboriously move, but as he didn't want to be alone at home, he joined others with all hardships.

Going there was like a picnic for everybody except Edgar and Lisa. As they entered the village, Edgar's mind started to go to past times. He could remember everything in details. Nothing was forgotten for him.

Lisa was immersed in looking around herself. She looked at everything accurately. She looked at houses, at trees, at gardens, at flowers, and everything she could see. She had never felt comfortable alike ever before. She could feel her motherland with all her heart. Flowers had a new scent for her.

Edgar was looking for his own house. Some houses were still in ruin. The village was not exactly the same as he last saw it. It had changed its face. Some new houses were built. Suddenly, he burst into tears when he found his own house.

They didn't expect anyone to live there. But the house was clean. It seemed that another family was living there. They went closer and ringed the bell. No one opened the door. There was a way to back yard. They went around the home and entered the back yard. Edgar was in front of others and Lisa behind him. Edgar sat on his knees and cried loudly and pointed to the corner of the garden. The flood of cry washed his face.

There were an old man and woman on wheelchairs. They were watering the flowers hand in hand …

March 4, 2009